CRUISE INTO EDEN

CRUISE INTO EDEN

LEXI POST

Acknowledgments

To Bob Fabich, my very own "beloved." For my sister Paige Wood, whose keen intellect keeps me on the right track.

Thank you to Merritt Crowder whose sharp eye and reading expertise is so valuable to my work. And thank you to my critique partner, Marie Patrick, for delaying her own work to help me improve mine. You're the best!

Author's Note

Cruise into Eden was inspired by Emily Dickinson's poem, *Wild nights! Wild nights!*, written in 1861 and published posthumously in the early 1890s. Unlike many of the writer's poems about death, here she fixates on passion. An interesting shift in focus for the extremely reclusive poet.

But what if the secretive Dickinson purposely disappeared from her writing desk to visit another planet by the name of Eden? Would her poetry then mean something else entirely? Would her legacy be alive there as well as here?

Wild nights! Wild nights!
Were I with thee,
Wild nights should be
Our luxury!

Futile the winds
To a heart in port, —
Done with the compass,
Done with the chart.

Rowing in Eden!
Ah! the sea!
Might I but moor
To-night in thee!

CHAPTER ONE

What had she been thinking to come on a nude cruise?

Erin Danielson maneuvered around the naked people sunning themselves on the deck above the pool, the drone of her mother's voice on her cell phone like white noise in the background of her growing uneasiness. Ascending the stairs to yet another deck, she moved the phone away from her face and sighed in relief as five empty lounge chairs came into view. She brought the phone back. "I'm sure she didn't mean it, Mom. Maybe you took it the wrong way."

Dropping onto the lounge at the end, she tried to keep track of her mother's story, but it was hard to concentrate after all the stares she'd just received. Some people found her sexy new bikini funny, while others looked baffled.

"Erin. Erin. Did you hear that?"

"I'm sorry, Mom. I was distracted for a moment."

"I need you to listen to me. Here I am telling you about the worst insult I've ever had in my life and you— Oh, I have to go, Janice is calling. I'll call you back later."

"But I might not have cell—" The silence on the other end made it clear her mom was long gone. Tucking her phone into her bag, Erin spread her towel and pulled out the coconut 50 SPF suntan lotion. She didn't want to burn on the first full day.

She should never have let Craig talk her into coming on this nude cruise with him. It wasn't as if he was interested in her, not in that way. He had needed her in order to come aboard since it was for couples only, but they were just friends, had been friends for years, like every other man she'd met since she was seventeen. Thank God she'd lost her virginity before then because an eleven-year dry spell had made her desperate enough as it was. Then again, maybe it would have been better if she'd never known what she was missing.

As she covered her legs with lotion, the scent distracted her from her ruminations. She was proud of her legs, but to be fair she had her mom and her running to thank for them. The coconut fragrance had her envisioning warm tropical beaches with aqua-blue waters and maybe a cabana boy. Yes, definitely a hunk of male to fulfill her every need. She shook her head. The chances of that happening were equal to her finding a wormhole on the Lido Deck, and yet she still held out hope.

She couldn't completely blame Craig for her being on the cruise. She'd come aboard for one last attempt. If she couldn't get a man interested in having sex with her on a nude cruise, she would give up the hunt. Besides, this new adventure seemed better than jetting off to Cancun for the eighth time with her friends. She'd lost two of those friends because of her decision to go with Craig. They acted as if they couldn't plan the vacation without her, while they had no problem with Craig backing out.

She smoothed lotion over her flat stomach, shaking her head. Craig, who she'd seen naked in college too many times, was a little too self-involved for her taste. She and her friends were sure the only reason he got drunk was for an excuse to take off his clothes. It didn't surprise her that he wanted to come on a nude cruise.

The least he could have done was come outside with her to rub lotion on her back. He'd never find her two decks above the pool. Last night at dinner, he hadn't stopped scanning the crowd once. Everyone had dressed for the meal, but some of the clothing revealed more than it hid and he had enjoyed the views. This morning he left the cabin butt-naked, and she hadn't seen him since.

She glanced down between the railings at the naked bodies below. The term "clothing optional" cruise was obviously a misnomer. Everyone was naked. Everyone. Old, young, fat, thin, even those with missing parts and scars. She had expected a lot of buff, model-type people, but they weren't. They were like the people she met at home, except they didn't have any clothes on.

It hadn't occurred to her to actually walk around nude. She stood out simply because she chose the "option" of wearing her bright-yellow bikini. She'd never expected to feel uncomfortable because she had her clothes *on*.

She reached over her shoulder as best she could to rub the lotion in. Sighing, she gave up and put it back in her bag and lay down. The motion of the ship was almost nonexistent, but if she concentrated hard, she could feel a slight side-to-side movement as the giant white playground slid through the water. Up this high, the noises from the pool and waterslide were muffled, leaving her in a peaceful haven.

"Excuse me, but are these taken?"

Shading her face with her hand, she opened her eyes to find the most gorgeous man she could imagine, because she was sure she hadn't actually seen a person so perfect. It was as if she'd stepped into a long-lost episode of *Star Trek* and the crew had just discovered heaven. He had to be well over six feet tall. His short, wavy brown hair was a bit messed from the breeze and his dark eyes were set above a perfect, straight nose. His lips curved in a grin that could melt the polar ice cap, and was definitely causing her own temperature to rise. The dark stubble along his chin gave him a rugged look that said he had a bit more testosterone than she was usually treated to. He appeared to have a round tattoo of some kind on his left biceps, but she couldn't tell what it was from where she sat. She let her gaze move lower to find large pectoral muscles with no sign of hair followed by a six-pack a bodybuilder would kill for.

She couldn't help but look lower only to flush at the sight of a very large cock nestled above a significant ball sac. Snapping her gaze back to his face, she shook her head. "Hmm, uh, no, they aren't taken."

"Do you mind if we join you?" His deep, slightly accented voice brought her senses into hyperalert and it took her a moment to understand what he'd said.

"We?"

"Yes, my friend and me." He pointed to her right and she forced herself to stop looking at him only to find another feast for her eyes.

She had to be dreaming. Maybe she was in some kind of time warp and had been whisked away to another planet because there was no way men like this existed on Earth. The second man had long black hair and eyes that seemed lighter than the other's, but she couldn't tell the color because the sun was behind him. His cheekbones were high and his chin sharper than his companion's. His lips, however, were distinctively full, which had her licking her own. Luckily, he didn't smile and simply nodded once.

The sun suddenly became stifling, so she sat up. "Of course you can join me." She stared as the long-haired man walked around the other one, lifted a lounge chair with his free hand and bent over to set it on the other side of her, giving her a view of the back of his taut thigh muscles, ass, and balls. Holy shit. She might come just looking at these two.

Wait. If these two men were together, they must be a couple. Her blood cooled. Damn, just her luck.

"My name is Nassic Wild, but everyone calls me Nase." The first man held out his hand.

She grasped it silently, still reeling from the man's attractiveness and his unobtainability.

Nase grinned. "My friend is Wareson Night, but we call him Ware."

She looked at the other man, who once again simply nodded. "Ware? Like in Werewolf?"

Nase laughed. "There's no such thing as a werewolf."

She attempted a smile, still too blown away by their physicality to be sure she succeeded.

"And you are?"

Nase's voice sent her senses into hyper mode. "Oh, I'm sorry. I'm Erin Danielson."

The man's gaze shifted to Ware for a moment before he looked at her again. "It's nice to *meet* you, Erin."

Now what was that about? He said the word "meet" as if he'd heard of her, but that couldn't be. Unless Craig had sent them up to show her what she couldn't have. If he'd done that, she would kick him out of their stateroom so fast he'd skin his bare ass on the doorsill on his way out.

Nase stepped in front of her, blocking the sun for a moment, helping her body to cool a bit. "I'm going to the bar to grab a couple beers. Would you like anything?"

"I would love a bottled water."

"A bucket of beers and a couple waters on the way." Nase strode off, completely comfortable in his nudity, and Erin completely comfortable with the view of his rounded backside.

She glanced at Ware, who now sat on the lounge chair next to her rubbing lotion on his bulging biceps. Above those massive muscles on his right shoulder was what looked like natural beauty marks, but they were in an odd shape, two dots in a row above three dots in a row. Despite the fact the man was as dark as someone from Greece, they stood out clearly. How odd.

She stared as Ware protected his skin, *all* of his skin. The man had no tan lines. He was a bit bigger than Nase, and broader, but not by much. He still hadn't said anything, and she suddenly wanted to hear his voice. "Have you taken a nude cruise before?"

He stilled mid-rub and looked at her. His gaze was intense and now that he was next to her, she could see his eyes were a forest green. Absolutely breathtaking, though it could have been her anticipation of his voice that had her holding her breath.

"No. This is our first one."

The deepness of his tone wrapped around her like a cocoon that she never wanted to leave. His accent was heavier, but from where? The tension she felt around Nase disappeared with Ware, which left her clearheaded enough to remember the two men were a couple and she had no right to ogle them. "This is my first one, too. Though I'm not sure I will ever get into the 'nude' part." She forced herself to stop staring at Ware's perfect male body. She closed her eyes and lay back on her lounge.

"Why?"

The dark, sensuous voice slid over her skin again, and she could feel him looking at her. No, not looking, exploring her with his sight. She opened her eyes and watched him. Every place he viewed suddenly became sensitized, as if he had lightly run his fingers along her body. She swore she could feel his gaze as it traveled across her stomach, up her ribs, over her breasts, along her neck, and through her hair until she found his eyes riveted on hers. "Why?"

"Yes. Why would you not allow your body to enjoy the sun fully?"

She pushed her hair behind her ear. "I... I—It's hard to explain."

He cocked his head and stared intently at her.

Obviously her answer had not satisfied him. "I'm guessing you are not American. In my country, we wear clothes all the time. It's what we're used to. I know there are a few countries that are more open about nakedness, but I'm not from those."

"I believe many of the people on this ship are from America."

Erin was too focused on the extra emphasis he left on the final letter "a" in "America" to at first grasp his point. When she did, she flushed. "True, but I never knew they existed. This is all very new to me. I just learned last night why there are piles of towels in the main areas of the boat. I guess everyone is supposed to use them to sit on if they are nude. I'm sure I'll learn a lot more about this by the end of the week."

As if her answer had pleased him, he went back to rubbing lotion on his dark body. She couldn't help but watch as he finished covering his hard stomach, but as his hand dipped between his legs, she closed her eyes tight. The last thing she needed was to have an orgasm watching a gay man put on suntan lotion. Luckily, Craig had stayed out late last night, so she'd been able to pleasure herself. Maybe she should be a bit more appreciative of her roommate's habits.

She sensed Nase's return and opened her eyes. Shielding her face, she swallowed hard. The man moved with confidence. It was as if the air parted before him. If she were air, she would stand in his way and let him push that large cock, that swayed as he walked, right up against her. His thigh muscles rippled as he strode and too soon he had dropped onto the lounge next to her.

"Here you are. One bottled water for now and another in the bucket for later." He held out the water. She sat up and shook off the condensation before opening it. Taking a gulp, the cold liquid glided down her throat, cooling her a bit until it hit her stomach.

"Ware." Nase lobbed an open bottle of Heineken over her to his friend who caught it effortlessly, not a drop spilled. These two had obviously been together a long time. She wanted to know more, but it would be a waste of time. The cruise rules were everyone had to be with someone. The organizers did not want people coming on the cruise to try to hook-up. That's why Craig had needed her, so he could pretend he was part of a couple. She'd like to think the men flanking her had done the same thing, but she doubted it. They were too familiar with each other.

Nase opened another beer, a foreign brand she didn't recognize and took a few swallows. The cords in his neck moved as he chugged the liquid. His tanned skin glistened with sweat and she licked her lips to keep herself from licking him. When he brought the bottle down, he faced her, his legs spread wide, his cock on display.

Sunglasses. Why had she left her sunglasses in the room? She just wouldn't look. It would be impolite.

"So what is your life like?" Nase leaned his elbows on his knees, distracting her from his question for a moment. His tight forearms sprinkled with dark hair had her body revving.

A low noise from her other side returned her attention to the topic. "My life? Do you mean what I do for a living?"

Nase shrugged, and took another sip of beer.

"I'm an IT manager for a science fiction television station that sells stuff online. Actually, it's more like a district manager as my boss has many product centers under his purview and I'm his right-hand man. It's a good job that I can leave at the office. What about you?"

Nase grinned. "I'm in defense, but I can't talk about it." He gestured toward Ware with his beer. "He's in government. Very into laws and justice and what's fair."

Erin turned to find Ware on his back watching her. She took another sip of water. "So I guess you do take your work home."

"Always," Nase grumbled. "That man is always thinking. He needs to have more fun. Maybe on this cruise."

She nodded halfheartedly. Yup, they were definitely a couple. It was too heartbreaking to contemplate any further. Taking another sip of water, she capped her bottle and lay back on the lounge chair.

"Why do you wear clothes?"

She opened one eye and looked at Nase. She wanted to be irritated, but he was just too attractive to be mad at. "I'm exercising the option to be clothed."

At her answer, his brows lowered. "But you're gorgeous. Stunning. And you have a sexy body. I would think you would be proud to show it."

She flushed from the inside out at his words.

"And I bet your breasts are perfectly round with strong, hard nipples that beg to be sucked."

Even as moisture gathered between her legs, Ware interrupted. "Nase." The single word said low and sternly was enough. The other man shook his head in puzzlement and settled in to apply lotion to his own taut body.

Erin closed her eyes tightly and tried to relax. How could she let a gay man make her wet? She must be more desperate than she realized. But to be fair, the men on either side of her were sinfully built and no one could blame her.

Wait. Why were they on either side of her? If they were a couple, wouldn't they want to be next to each other? Then again, they could simply be protecting her. She had a couple gay friends who would do that, kind of look out for her. That must be it. Still, she could certainly dream if she wanted to, and she would, next time she had the chance to relieve her fast-growing sexual need.

CHAPTER TWO

Ware shook his head as they entered their cabin. "Strong, hard nipples that beg to be sucked? What were you thinking?"

Nase threw his hands up. "At least I didn't touch her. We've watched her for so long, I wanted to touch her, but I didn't. Do you know how hard that was for me? "

"Yeah, I do." Ware dropped his towel on the couch and sat on it. Seeing Erin in person had been overpowering, but it was more than her svelte body that had him fisting his hands to keep them by his sides. Her gaze was so open and her expression so readable, he'd wanted to take her in his arms and keep her safe.

"You do? It didn't look like you were struggling to stay away."

He stared at the ocean through the floor-to-ceiling glass doors of their suite, avoiding Nase's gaze. "I was. She was more than I expected and I was tempted to touch her. Her skin looked so soft. Just to hold her hand or feel that thick platinum hair on my shoulder would have been enough."

"Maybe for you, but not for me." Nase began to pace. "She's taller than I thought. Did you see her legs? So long. And her breasts," his hands clenched and released, "they would be a perfect handful. We need to release her pheromones, take her, make her ours."

Ware watched Nase, his movements like a wild animal in a cage, anxious yet determined. "We don't know enough about her yet. She may not be ready."

"Are you serious? The poor woman hasn't had sex with a male since she came of age and you think she isn't ready? I could practically smell her need. Trust me, she's ready."

Ware contemplated Nase's statement. He too had sensed her readiness, but that wasn't what he meant and Nase knew it. "We agreed to meet her and see how open she would be to our lives."

Nase stopped and faced him. "Yes. And if she is open, we agreed we would bring her home."

"I still don't think it's a good time."

"Ware, you will never think it's a good time while we live outside the city, but I'm telling you, if we don't bring her home, the men will begin to desert us. We can't take over the city without a strike force. She has to come back with us."

"I did not agree we should take her back to Naralina. The jungle is plentiful, and our compound walls become stronger every day."

Nase shook his head. "I can't believe you are talking about accepting our ostracism again. We don't deserve it. It was a setup. Just let me near Grandall and he will confess his deceitful actions."

Ware looked down at his hands. "That's exactly why he had to be rid of us both. He knew if you stayed, he'd be found out. We should have seen his duplicity and stopped it. But we were too complacent. Our naiveté cost us our positions and our homes.

As leaders, we should have been more alert. We deserved to be banished."

"No." Nase started to pace again. "I refuse to accept responsibility for someone else's machinations and lies. Grandall needs to be removed."

"Nase, don't you wonder at how easily the others accepted the accusations that we planned to steal women from Earth without their consent? Why wouldn't Rohert and Algeron have argued? They knew we were planning a new experiment with the discoverists to determine if the lack of females born was due to the planet or our genetics. They knew if we were successful there would be no reason to take women from Earth and yet they didn't say a word. There was a lot more happening than we knew."

"I make no excuse for being honest and expecting others to be as well. As far as I'm concerned, that's not a failing in me, but in others."

Ware couldn't argue that point. Nase was right. The others had failed the law, but his gut told him something deeper than mere competitiveness had fueled his and Nase's ousting. "And you want to bring Erin into this?" How could they possibly protect her?

"What I want is for us to do what we planned to do years ago. We are entitled to her. We chose her eleven years ago. We have the blessing of the High Poetess. And quite frankly, we need her."

He smirked at his friend's constant movement. Nase never could stay still. Even the day they had finally stepped on Earth to test Erin. They had found her because of her growing interest in stories about other planets, the way most Edenists targeted possible agapaytos. As they watched her, they admired her unending willingness to help others, but when they discovered her love for their planet's first High Poetess, they arranged to see her in person.

Nase had twitched as he tried to remain quiet while they watched Erin find the Dickinson poem they had left as a gift. She'd taken it from the poet's bedroom and scurried away. They knew then, they had made the right choice. Now she had to choose them in return. "We cannot force her. Then we would be doing exactly what Grandall accused us of." Ware leaned forward. "Any female must be willing."

Nase spun and flopped down on the recliner. "You don't have to quote Dickinson Law to me. I would never force her, but I'm not above trying a little seduction."

Ware shook his head at Nase's grin. Emily Dickinson had been quite aware of the sexual prowess of Edenists when she'd saved their world. It was one of the reasons she'd crafted her laws so carefully—to protect women from men with Nase's charm. "It's far more than that. We need to discover how open-minded Erin is. Men from another planet are not an everyday occurrence for Earth humans. We need to know what makes her happy."

Nase wiggled his brows. "Don't you think we could make her happy?"

"Yes, I do. But my concern is, can we keep her safe if we bring her home? We have not watched her every minute of her life. Checking on her through the portal does not mean we know her. We need to know she'll survive." *I need to know she will survive.*

"We certainly can't leave her here if we bond with her. And we plan on doing exactly that."

Ware moved his gaze back to the ocean, its changing blues and greens as the sun reflected off it reminding him of Erin's mixed eye color, beautiful, so expressive. Nase was right. As much as he didn't want to bring her back to their home in the jungle far outside the walls of Naralina, he could never leave her here now that he'd spoken to her, felt her essence, air-touched her body. She was like an addictive drug and he feared their addiction. If it was suddenly taken away, they would be powerless.

Nase interrupted his disturbing thoughts. "Do we agree? Shall I release her pheromones?"

Ware rose, a need for sweets rising in his gut. He walked into the kitchen area and unwrapped a plate of cookies. "What about this man she is rooming with? If you release her pheromones, and they are in close quarters with her in such need, she may turn to him."

"You're right. We need to free her when we are near." Nase stalked into the kitchen and grabbed up a couple cookies as well. "Tonight, after the dinner service."

Ware grabbed Nase's forearm as he moved it to bite into the sweet. "Once we do this, we still must allow her to choose."

The seriousness of what they were about to do penetrated Nase's need and he nodded solemnly. Ware let him go and headed for the shower. They had a long week of exploration ahead. A week he both anticipated and dreaded. At least he had the best friend an Edenist could have at his side. It may take everything they had to bring Erin home.

* * * * *

Erin took a sip of her wine and watched as Craig talked up a blonde woman halfway down the bar. She'd always considered him well built, but after meeting Nase and Ware, everyone on the ship paled in comparison, literally. In addition to their perfect physique, it was as if the two men lived on a nude cruise. They were dark all over.

Craig's arm slipped behind the busty woman who wore a revealing backless dress. Clearly, he was making progress. At least tonight she wasn't the only one clothed, though the dress was minimal. The men were generally nude, happy to leave their clothes behind after dinner, but many of the women wore outfits that made them appear sexy. She'd gone out on a limb and left her underclothes in her cabin, so she was naked beneath her dress. Though she doubted that counted. She smiled kindly at an older woman in the corner with her husband. She was naked, but she had a shawl over her shoulders against the chill of the air-conditioning. Erin envied her for being so comfortable in her skin, wrinkles, sags and all.

So why couldn't she be? That was the question Ware had asked her. Why couldn't she simply drop her clothes? Before dressing, she'd looked at herself in the full-length mirror screwed onto the cabin's bathroom door. Her figure was fine and she had no terrible scars or marks, not that people on the ship seemed to care. For a twenty-eight year-old, she was in very good shape. So why not get naked?

It was a question she'd contemplated again over dinner when she noticed Ware and Nase at a table not far from her own. The cruise line rules were that no one was allowed to eat dinner naked. She assumed it was a food-service thing. Nase and Ware had worn loose beige tops and white cotton pants like she'd expect to see in the Caribbean. Though the clothes had hidden their assets, it brought more focus to their beautifully sculpted faces, and she'd seen more than one woman sigh and shake her head as they left the dining room.

A vibration in her purse surprised her. Weren't they out of cell range yet? She hated to admit it, but she looked forward to being unreachable. She pulled out her phone. Ernest Jacobs' name greeted her and she slid her finger across the screen. "You know I'm on vacation, right?"

"Hello to you too, Erin. You can't expect to leave for a week and have everything run smoothly. We need the password for the router."

She lifted her glass and took a soothing sip of wine. "Ernest, I left you a printout of all the key passwords, which you know already, plus I emailed them to you."

"I wouldn't be calling you if I could find the email. Where did you put the printout?"

"It's in your top right drawer in a green folder. If that's all, I really have to go."

"Right drawer. Okay. What day will you be back in the office? We have the new contract to get out by the end of the month. You will be back to go over that, right?"

"Ernest, I have to go. I left you everything you need. I'm on vacation with somebody. Goodbye."

Ending the call, she shivered. She'd never hung up on her boss before. She must be more stressed than she realized to have done that. Every time he was promoted, he'd taken her right along with him. She should be grateful, not hanging up on him.

Picking up her wine again, her hand shook. At least if she spilled the deep burgundy it shouldn't show, since her dress matched the wine's color perfectly. She liked the formfitting spaghetti strap dress that just covered her ass. All part of her brilliant plan to have sex while on the cruise.

She twirled the glass as she scanned the room carefully. Many people were in pairs. Unlike Craig, it appeared the passengers really were couples on this cruise, which dropped her chances of getting laid from minimal to nil. She looked down at her half-empty glass. How much wine would she need to consume to forget she'd wasted her vacation time on a nude cruise with no chance of sex?

At least she wasn't home watching Season 7 of Dr. Who, again. She'd never get laid doing that, though it was a good consolation plan. Sighing, she put the glass on the bar and turned toward the room again, only to find Nase standing in front of her. "Oh, hi."

"Hi. We were looking for you."

At his use of the ever present "we," she swiveled around and found Ware behind her. Again they sandwiched her. *If only.* "You were looking for me? Why?"

"We thought you might like to go dancing."

Dancing? She'd seen gay men dancing together the first night of the cruise, so why would they ask her? And why the hell was she hesitating? "I'd love to dance. Which club has dancing?"

Nase lifted her wineglass before holding out his arm. "Follow me and I promise not to lead you astray."

A distinctive grunt came from behind her, but before she could turn to look at Ware, Nase had pulled her forward. She didn't have to see Ware to sense his presence and smell the distinctive scent that was all his. It was a slightly sweet, almost banana-like aroma that made her want to eat. She had noticed it on deck, but thought it was the suntan lotion. That it was a part of him made her more curious.

She addressed Nase, whose own scent reminded her of freshly washed linen. "You never did tell me where you two are from."

"We live near a naked city. Have you heard of it?"

"Actually, just this evening. Someone at our table told us about it. They said it was in the south of France. I can't imagine a whole city of naked people. So you go out to dinner naked? Go shopping naked? Even go to work naked?"

Nase halted them in front of a bank of elevators. "Of course. Anytime you would like to see it, I would be happy to bring you there."

Ware's deep voice coming from behind her was stern. "Nase."

"What?" He didn't look back as he smiled down at her. "I'm just offering."

The elevator doors opened and Nase guided her in. Ware followed, stepping behind them once again. As the doors closed, a soft sensation glided over her ass as if someone touched it softly. She looked over her shoulder to see Ware standing with his arms folded across his chest and his gaze lowered. Now she was hallucinating. Did she want sex so badly she could make herself feel as if someone touched her?

Nase squeezed her arm in the crook of his. "Everything okay?"

She flushed. "Yes, fine." She needed a distraction. Anything to stop thinking of these men as possible lovers. Her gaze flitted toward Nase and caught upon the tattoo on his biceps, but it wasn't the color of any tattoo she'd ever seen. It was the color of a dark freckle, but it was clearly a spiral. "Your tattoo could make someone dizzy."

Nase's brows lowered in confusion before he glanced at his arm. "Oh. Yes. I know."

That went about as far as warp a engine with no anti-matter. Again she felt as if Ware stroked her ass. It had to be the air flow in the elevator. She was pathetic. "Could I have a sip of my wine?"

"Of course." Nase brought the glass to her lips, the gesture intimate. What would Ware think? She grasped the stem around Nase's hand. Heat seared through her palm, up her arm and straight down to her pussy, causing her to tilt the wine a bit more than planned and she gulped the liquid down. Letting go as if stung, she looked back at Ware, whose gaze focused on her mouth.

He raised his hand and without a word, used his finger to wipe away a small drop at the corner of her lips. Then he licked his finger clean.

Erin snapped her head back to the front of the elevator just as the doors opened and Nase led her forward. Her mind spun from Ware's erotic gesture even as her body heated.

The air-conditioning blast as they entered the large, round room chilled her quickly, and she shivered.

Nase handed the wineglass to Ware. "Here, I need to get this woman on the dance floor to warm her up."

She ran her hand down her arm to erase the goose bumps. "What? No, it's okay. It was—"

Nase grabbed her hand and pulled her as fast as her four-inch, ankle-strapped heels allowed. When they hit the dance floor, he immediately twirled her around and moved her to the pounding rhythm of the music. She couldn't help but catch his excitement and moved with him. Releasing her hand, he showed her enough hip action to make her drool. So not fair. To retaliate, she did the same, though it was probably wasted on him, but there could be others watching. Who knew? Maybe dancing with one man would bring up the competitive instincts in another. She was willing to try anything.

Besides, Nase was an awesome dancer, by himself or partnering her. He led her through three heart-pounding dances before she finally refused to continue. "I need a breather and a drink."

"Right." Linking his fingers with hers, he led her off the floor to a darkened alcove where Ware patiently waited. As they approached, she noticed Ware had taken his clothes off and now sat on them. She groaned at the sight of his muscled thighs, thankful the music was too loud for Nase to have heard. Would he be angry if he caught her ogling his man?

Nase had her precede him behind the tiny cocktail table on the curved couch. She slid in, not quite touching Ware and pushed her hair back behind her ears. What she wouldn't do for a hair clip. Too bad cruise ships didn't have replicators.

Nase divested himself of his own clothes and laid them on the couch next to her before dropping down to sit against her. Again she looked to Ware, who was in the process of shifting closer. What was going on?

"Did you want to undress as well?" Nase slid his finger under her spaghetti strap and stroked her shoulder playfully. The shiver of excitement that raced through her was noticed, and he grinned before dropping a kiss on her skin. The heat he left behind flowed through her body.

That was it. She couldn't take any more. "What are you doing?"

"What do you mean?" Nase removed his hand, obviously trying to look hurt.

"Why have you brought me here? Didn't you two come here to spend time together? Why do you keep including me? And why are you kissing me when you—you are not interested. I have to tell you, it isn't fair."

Ware's hand on her two tightly clasped ones calmed her frazzled sexual need. "We are not here to spend time with each other. We are not gay. I'm sorry if we led you to believe otherwise. That was not our intention."

Not gay? She stared into Ware's understanding gaze. They weren't gay. And they had sandwiched her once again. Oh God. Her heart raced at the possibilities.

Ware's thumb stroked over the back of her hand, slowing her heart rate and bringing her brain back on track. Here she was with two amazingly male men, and they were both interested in her. Would she have to choose?

Ware let go of her and stood, holding his hand out. "Come. Dance with me."

The blaring, pounding music had stopped and a slow melody had taken its place. She looked at Nase, who simply nodded. Taking Ware's hand, she stood and followed him as he guided her onto the floor. As soon as his arms came around her, she felt safe, cared for, supported, all the things she'd always given to others but had never received. Oh God, where did that come from?

Ware must have sensed her agitation because he started to stroke her back as they swayed to the music's rhythm. He held her tight, but did not press himself into her. His voiced soothed her. "You have many questions."

She nodded against his shoulder, vaguely wondering how short she would feel with him if she wasn't in her heels.

"I think the one you are most curious about is why we are spending time with you. The truth is we would like to have sex with you, but it is your choice."

Erin leaned her head back to stare at the strange man holding her in his arms. His accent made him sound so sexy, but she had to see the truth in his eyes. It had been eleven long years with no men interested in her that way. Many male friends and numerous blind dates, but no one had wanted her in their bed. Now, she was to believe these two muscle-bound men wanted her?

"So you both want to have sex with me and are okay with sharing?"

"Yes." Ware's resolute stare had her believing him. Maybe she wanted to too much.

"Why?"

Ware's slight smile had her catching her breath. It couldn't even really be considered a true smile, but just a slight lifting of the corners of his mouth. Yet it made her feel as if the sun had risen in the middle of the night.

His eyes softened. "Because you are the one for us."

She laid her head back on his shoulder. He could have said anything, that she was sexy, that she was pretty, that she made Nase laugh or him feel protective. But he didn't say any of that. No, simply that she was the one for them and somehow that meant so much more.

She tensed. Did that mean more than a cruise fling?

Ware eased his hand down her back and gently pressed her hips closer to him. The feel of his hard cock against her mons through the skintight dress caused her pussy to swell. Suddenly, all that mattered was that he wanted her.

The sound of a fast-beat song woke her from her sexual haze and she found herself being walked back to Nase.

"Are you ready for more wine?"

"Actually, I think I'd like a ginger ale." As she scooted back behind the cocktail table, she caught Nase sharing a nod with Ware. Had these two been together so long they knew what each other thought?

Ware lifted her hand and gave it a kiss that melted her heart. "We will return. Remember, it is your choice."

As the two men walked away, she couldn't help sighing at their tight asses. She really didn't have to make a choice. If they wanted to share her, she was all for it. The question was, how could she hint she wanted to go back to their room sooner rather than later? Then again, they had been very blunt, so maybe she should be as well.

"Excuse me. But would you care to dance?"

Erin looked up to find a naked blond man with a shaved chest and genital area leaning toward her. He smiled, showing perfect white teeth.

She looked over her shoulder, but no one was there. Oh duh, of course, he spoke to her. Wait. No one ever asked *her* to dance… except Nase and Ware.

He extended his hand. "I'm sorry, I should introduce myself. I'm Glen, and you are?"

"I'm Erin."

"Nice to meet you. Would you like to dance?"

She scanned the bar area for Ware and Nase, but couldn't find them. "I'm actually here with someone."

"I'm sure he won't mind. It's just a dance."

She focused on the pounding music. Ware had said it was her choice. "I'd be happy to."

Dancing with Glen was fun, though his moves weren't exactly in time to the music. Just the fact a handsome man asked her to dance had her walking on air. First Ware and Nase wanted to have sex with her and now this man had asked her to dance. Maybe it was the dress. Either that or she unknowingly drank an irresistible potion from a *Stargate* episode.

No sooner had Glen returned her to her seat when another man approached her. Carlos requested a dance as well. The Latin man was well built and could dance better than she could.

By the time she sat again, Herve introduced himself and asked for a dance.

"I think I need a moment. Would you mind sitting this one out?"

Herve's German accent was heavy, but he spoke very good English. "I will sit with you then." As he walked across the room to retrieve his towel so he could join her, another man approached. She'd never had so much attention of this type in her life. Maybe her luck had changed.

Nase growled. "That's the fifth man. Look at them. They're practically drooling over her."

"And you weren't?"

"I don't drool." He gritted his teeth in frustration. Seeing Erin with men vying for her attention had his nerves on edge. She was his and Ware's. Only they had the right to have her, but her pert nose and sweet face was attracting every man in the bar. He was the one who had stifled her pheromones when she was seventeen and he was the one who had released them. "You could have told me you revealed our need for her *before* I removed the block on her pheromones."

"No, I couldn't. If I had, you wouldn't have removed it and she must *choose* us, not take us because we are her only option."

Nase fisted his hands, unable to refute Ware's point. Not only was he right according to Dickinson Law, but also according to what their woman deserved. Still, it rankled. They had watched her grow, seen her successes and failures even as they had their own. She was *theirs*. "I need a shot."

Ware shook his head. "Here. Have a beer. Just be thankful this isn't the seventh deck. She'll be fine."

Nase grabbed the cold bottle from his friend and gulped down half of it. It didn't help. If Ware expected him to stand by and not do bodily harm to at least three men, he would need something a lot stronger. "So exactly when do I get to knock down a few of these males?"

"When she is ready for us."

"What? We already discussed this. She is ready for us."

Ware tilted his beer bottle back and took a telling swallow.

Witnessing his controlled friend's obvious stress had Nase calming. Not much could get under Ware's skin, but if *he* was having trouble, Nase felt a whole lot better that he'd had to tamp down his own inclinations.

Ware brought the bottle down. "What I meant was, we will know when she makes her decision."

"And you think standing over here is going to keep us in her mind?"

"She deserves this admiration. We have denied her for so long, perhaps too long." Ware's brows lowered. "Look, she is practically breathing in the attention."

Nase watched Erin. She sat on the couch with a man on either side of her and two more standing in front of her. From his angle, he couldn't see her face, but beneath the table he watched her crossed leg moving up and down. The thought of her uncrossing her legs and showing him the entrance to her sheath had him taking another swallow of beer.

Despite the need to slam down the bottle, he kept himself in check and set it on the bar then ordered a whiskey, ignoring Ware's disappointed stare. He wouldn't even pretend to have the control Ware had, nor did he need to. He was a man of action, Ware a man of thought. Together, they were perfect for Erin.

He stared again at her long, smooth legs. Her calves had an enticing bulge that reminded him of her years on the track team and her hours spent on a treadmill. The woman could run.

One of the men moved, blocking his view, forcing him to notice the hard-on. No, not one but three hard cocks. "Shit."

CHAPTER THREE

"What is it?" Ware's calm irritated Nase, as usual.

"At least three of those men are erect just talking to her."

"Yes."

Nase turned away from the view of Erin to look at his friend. "I think it's time we joined her growing crowd."

When Ware didn't respond immediately, Nase studied his friend. Ware had grasped the wrought iron back of the barstool next to him and bent it out of shape. Nase grinned. To watch Ware in a fight was a pleasure, but to see his restraint faltering was downright satisfying. "Hey, Ware. Relax. They're just humans."

Ware breathed in noisily and slowly let the air out as he peeled his fingers from the iron. "Technically, we are humans too."

Nase disagreed, but didn't say anything. As far as he was concerned, they were advanced humans at the least. The Crius had taken their ancestors from ancient Greece over a thousand years ago and they had evolved differently on Eden. They were Edenists and superior in too many ways to count…except for their inability to have female children. "Are you ready to go back to our woman so she can choose us as her agapaytos?"

"Wait." Ware's hand on his arm caused him to look back at Erin. He could see her face now, and it was clear she was excited by all the attention, but her leg moved faster and she kept twirling her wineglass around and around.

"Damn." He swore under his breath. "If any of them has said anything to upset her..."

Ware's grip on his arm tightened. "I don't think it's the men's conversation. It may simply be all the attention at once. She's not used to it."

"I'm glad of that."

"There. There it is."

Nase focused on her face. She tucked her hair behind her right ear and looked directly at them, despite the men around her. "She wants us."

Ware let go of his arm. "No. She needs us. Grab her ginger ale. We don't want to keep her waiting."

Nase lifted the full glass from the bar and left his whiskey untouched. She'd chosen them. His relief loosened his insides and he found his grin returning as they moved back to their table. He slid her glass of ginger ale in front of her.

Erin smiled at him in gratefulness and his heart tripped in his chest. "Excuse us, gentlemen."

The men sitting next to Erin looked up and reluctantly took their towels and left. By the time he and Ware had arranged their clothes on the seat and sat again, the rest of the men had taken the hint.

Erin took a sip of her drink before setting it down, her leg no longer moving beneath the table. "I'm glad to see you two. Where did you go?"

Nase couldn't keep from touching her any longer and wrapped his arm around her shoulders.

Ware took her hand. "We saw you had company and didn't want to interrupt."

"I don't know what happened." Her brows lowered in confusion. "All of a sudden, they wanted to talk with me."

"Just talk?" Nase couldn't keep the growl from his voice and she turned her face toward him.

"No. They wanted more."

"Of course they did." He gazed at her substantial cleavage. "You are a very desirable woman."

Her blush beneath the changing colored lights was adorable, and he kissed her on the cheek.

Ware, damn him, had to probe. "And did you want more from them?"

Nase held his breath. Here was the beginning or the end to their relationship and his and Ware's leadership.

Erin looked at him and then Ware and back to him. "No. Maybe before I met you two, but now I only want you."

Erin didn't completely comprehend her sudden popularity, but at the moment she didn't care. All the male attention had made her dizzy. It was as if her body had revved itself into such a high pitch that it left her lightheaded. But she was on vacation and she had the two most attractive men on the ship wanting to have sex with her. That gave her a confidence she'd never experienced before. "Can we go back to your room?"

Nase's grin turned devilish and her heart soared. "Now that's my kind of woman. What do you say, Ware?"

She turned to Ware to find his gaze intense. He gave his signature nod and Nase stood, pulling her up with him.

"Let's go."

She shivered in anticipation. The fact that these two men were so anxious to take her to bed had her laughing as the three of them moved to the elevators. After a short ride up, Nase opened the door to their cabin, only it wasn't a cabin.

"This is huge." She unhooked her arm from Nase and dropped her purse on a couch as she approached the floor-to-ceiling windows. They had a living room, kitchen and two bedrooms from what she could see. And the balcony was the length of the living room. She touched the handle of the slider. "May I?"

"Of course." Nase moved to her side and opened the glass door. She stepped onto the wide balcony and the ocean breeze slid over her body. The area was lit with two red lamps, giving it a warm glow, and there was a queen sized lounge with thick cushions. Across from that were two chairs and in the other corner was another huge lounge. Small tables were scattered about.

Nase stepped behind her and wrapped his arms around her waist.

"Do you like it?"

She nodded. Her throat closed as his warm body pressed against hers.

Ware walked past them and laid a sheet over the large lounge before he put a towel on a chair opposite them and sat. He opened a bottle of water and took a gulp, the tendons in his neck distracting her as he swallowed.

Nase spoke against her ear. "Does the breeze flowing across your skin feel good?"

She focused on the brush of air the ship's passage created. It was a gentle, warm, steady touch against the entire front of her body. "It does. It's like a caress. No, like many caresses."

Nase unwound his arm and rested his hands on her shoulders. "Would you like to feel it on your breasts?"

Her heart skipped a beat and her pussy tightened at the idea. Could she? It wasn't as if the balcony were a public place. She glanced back at Nase. "Yes."

His look sent tingles racing across her skin. Slowly, he lifted her spaghetti straps off her shoulders, but the dress was so formfitting it didn't move. As he kissed her shoulder like he had in the night club, he pulled the front of the dress down over her breasts to her waist.

She let her head fall back as the moving air brushed against her skin, causing her nipples to pucker in yearning. Nase's hands remained on her waist as his lips moved to her neck. A stronger pressure on her nipples sent hot pleasure racing to her pussy and she opened her eyes to glance at her breasts. Her nipples were hard nubs, but Nase had not touched them. Was she so pathetic that the breeze could do that to her?

She moved her attention to Ware, who sat watching. His gaze was on her nipples and the sensation of them being rubbed started again. She gasped and he lifted his eyes to look at hers. It was as if he'd touched her just by looking at her, but that couldn't be. This wasn't her sci-fi channel. It was a very real nude cruise.

Nase chose that moment to push her dress down to her hips, baring her belly. She glanced at Ware and found him following Nase's progress with avid interest. She should be shy, but they were so into her, it made her feel beautiful. She didn't resist as

Nase pushed the dress past her hips until it dropped to the floor, revealing her own nakedness.

He growled in her ear. "Now I'm glad you covered up. I don't want anyone to see how gorgeous you are."

She grinned. "Now how can you tell when you're standing behind me?"

"Ah Fiya, you challenge me and I always accept a challenge."

"What?"

Before she understood what he meant, Nase had stepped away and stood next to Ware.

Her instinct was to cover up, but she forced her hands to remain at her sides while the two men viewed her from the top of her hair to the tops of her feet. Again, air lightly brushed her skin, just slightly stronger than the breeze of the ship's passage. The touch excited her and as it moved down past her belly, she grasped for a distraction. "What is Fiya?"

Nase's gaze moved to hers and the desire in his dark eyes had her limbs tingling.

Surprisingly, it was Ware who answered. "It's difficult to translate. It's an honorable endearment."

"I like the sound of it."

Ware looked to Nase. "I think Erin would like to come."

Nase grinned. "I can help with that."

This had to be the strangest intercourse ever. Then again, she didn't know much about it besides the few times she had sex when very young, and she definitely had never had it with two men. How would it work, exactly?

As Nase moved behind her again, she looked to Ware and found him studying her. He read her so well. Would he know she had no clue what to do? Did he sense she was very inexperienced despite her wish otherwise?

He lifted his water bottle in salute. "Erin, I'm going to watch as you find the *la petite mort*, as the French say."

His voice had her anxiety drifting away, leaving only her excitement. She vaguely wondered if he was a hypnotist, but was quickly distracted by Nase and his hands. He ran his fingers down her arms until he grasped hers.

Ware shifted in his chair. "Open your stance."

Kicking her dress to the side, she carefully moved her legs out a little wider than her shoulders, not daring to go farther as she still had her heels on.

Nase gently pulled her arms behind her back and held her wrists with one hand, arching her back slightly and pushing her breasts forward, like an offering to Ware. The breeze from the ship's progress continued to caress her skin, causing her anticipation to build.

Then she felt it again. A deliberate brush of air across her stomach. Her muscles reacted, tensing beneath it. She looked at Ware. *He* made that happen, but how?

The pressure moved upward, brushing over her breasts until it reached her nipples, where the air seemed to spiral in circles, making her nubs hard and causing sharp contractions between her thighs.

Ware lowered his gaze and the pressure moved downward, over her belly button and onto her pubic hair, which she kept shaved in the shape of a triangle pointing to her clit. She'd done so ten years earlier after reading an article in a woman's magazine that said men liked it that way, and she'd never stopped doing it…just in case. The pressure sifted through the small thatch of hair before it continued its downward path.

The air pushed against her clit and she moaned, tilting her hips forward, wanting more.

Nase's growl in her ear reminded her he was there, holding her wrists. She could do nothing to help herself reach climax and she wanted to. "Nase, please."

"I thought you'd never ask."

His lips pressed against her neck even as he used his free hand to cup her breast and stroke her nipple with his thumb. His touch was stronger than the movement between her legs and she needed it to match. "More."

At her word, the pressure against her clit strengthened as it moved up and down against her sensitive spot. She bent her legs to open them wider and the strokes elongated to her opening and back to her clit.

Nase's breathing came faster, feeding her excitement. She tried to release her hands, but instead he wrapped them around his large, hard cock. She couldn't resist squeezing him.

"Yes," he groaned as he pressed his body against hers, trapping her hands behind her. He wrapped his arms around her, crossing them to latch on to her nipples with his fingers. "Come for us, Fiya."

Oh God, that would be so easy. She let her head fall back against his shoulder and closed her eyes. Her breathing was fast, her body growing more tense by the minute as the strokes on her clit increased their rhythm. Nase's fingers sent bolts of excitement down to meet the tension in her pussy. She'd always had to do this for herself. To have a man, men, bring her release was overwhelming.

"What…about…you?" She could barely form the words between her pants.

Nase pinched her nipples, sending fire to her core, bringing her to the edge. "I will be inside you soon, but first Ware wants to see you come."

At that she opened her eyes to find Ware's gaze at her pussy. The need to grant his wish was strong. Knowing he watched her there made her clench.

Nase settled his chin atop her head. "Now."

The pressure on her clit suddenly changed, pushing hard as Nase tightened his fingers on her nipples. The dual sensations collided in her core and her world exploded. She rocked her hips forward as she bucked in ecstasy against the invisible pressure. Her head grew light and red lights swirled around her. Finally, she recognized something other than pure pleasure. Nase's arm, tight across her waist, holding her up.

Taking her own weight again, she found her arms free and steadied herself against him. "Oh my God, that was incredible."

His grin was full of pride. "Of course it was."

She lowered her brows, but could only hold the expression for so long. He was just too handsome and too right to argue with.

Nase looked past her. "Ware, did that meet with your approval?"

Erin turned to Ware, who sat back in his chair taking a sip of water. He looked calm, but his cock had risen up in response to her orgasm. Wait. He hadn't touched her. "How did you do that?"

He cocked his head slightly. "Do what?"

"Do you make the air move against me?"

He raised one brow. "Interesting and accurate description. It is a talent I have."

Okay, now this was strange. Not only could he do whatever it was he did to her, but he also admitted it. Why did she suddenly feel as if she'd entered a Farscape episode and eaten some tannot root?

"My turn." Without warning, Nase lifted her up and gently deposited her on the wide lounge. She lay on her back for a moment and simply admired the body of the man who would finally penetrate her after years of forced abstinence. His cock was thick and long and it was just a bit bigger than her favorite vibrator. To have him push into her, spread her wide, had her pussy growing wet all over again.

"Turn over."

She forced her gaze to his face. "You want me on my stomach?"

"No, I want you on all fours. I need to bury myself deep inside you, and Ware needs to see me do it."

More than willing, she did as Nase asked and presented her butt to him.

"By the Crius, I'm going to want that ass another day. Look at that, Ware."

Erin turned in time to see Ware lick his lips as he stared at her backside. She dropped her head, too charged up to take any more foreplay.

Nase stroked her ass first with his hands and then with his cock.

She wanted him inside her, now.

His finger traced her crease lightly, sending shivers along her arms before continuing downward to slip inside her sheath. "Yessss," she hissed.

"Are you ready, Erin?"

She nodded, her throat too tense with anticipation to say anything.

His finger pulled out and pushed her labia aside. The head of his cock touched her. She wanted to rush back against him and start moving, but her mind kicked into gear. "Wait."

Chapter Four

Nase stopped. "What's wrong?"

Erin collapsed on the bed. "We need protection."

"From what?" Nase looked over the balcony.

She rolled her eyes. "From STDs."

He glanced at Ware, who stared at her with a puzzled expression. Didn't they have STDs in France? They must. She was pretty sure they were all over the world. "You know, sexually transmitted diseases? We need a condom to protect us from one another."

Nase stepped back. "I don't have any of these diseases and neither does Ware." The man was so insulted that his beautiful hard-on softened.

"I'm not saying you do. But unless you've been tested, you can't be sure, which is why we use condoms. Besides, it is to protect you too. What if I had an STD?"

Ware lowered his brows. "You do not have a disease."

"I appreciate your confidence in me, but you can't be completely sure. Yes, I've been tested as it is my doctor's regular routine, but you haven't seen the results."

"Damn. Just tell us where to get this condom."

She stared at Nase. They really didn't know anything about this. Maybe she could visit them after the cruise because she was very curious about where they lived now. "I have some in my purse. I think I left it inside."

Nase stalked into the suite and she was left alone with Ware. He didn't look at her, but instead appeared to be pondering some great truth. The man certainly kept to himself. And yet, he was the one who told her they wanted to have sex with her, but he had only watched, or whatever it was he had done.

Nase came back outside and gave her the purse. Quickly, she opened it up and pulled out the biggest condom she had. A girl had to dream, and in this case, she had received more than she ever imagined.

"What do you do with that?"

She glanced up at Nase. "I put it on you."

"No."

"Yes."

He looked askance at the package in her hand.

"If you want to push that handsome cock into my wet pussy, you are going to have to bring yourself over here and let me roll this on you." She grinned as Nase's cock came to attention at that.

Still, he hesitated. "What does it do?"

She took a deep breath. Explaining a condom to these highly skilled, sexual men wasn't what she'd expected. "It just sticks tight to your skin. This way when you come, it will still keep us separate."

"But I don't want—"

"Nase." There it was, that one word said in a specific tone from Ware that had Nase walking toward her again.

She licked her lips. "First, I need to be sure you are hard enough." She grinned at his intake of breath and the way his cock twitched in front of her. Then she lightly licked the head.

"By the Crius woman, put it on before I ejaculate inside that pretty mouth of yours."

She could keep enjoying him, but she wanted him as much as he wanted her, only she'd been the one waiting longer. Quickly, she unrolled the condom as far as it would go. It didn't reach his base. Would it still work?

"Now on your hands and knees."

Nase's command caused an ache deep inside her pussy. To be wanted so much that he couldn't wait had her shaking with anticipation. She assumed the position quickly.

He once again rubbed her ass and sighed. "I'm going to want you over and over and over again. I can already tell."

He spoke to her but it was as if he talked to himself, which made his words crawl inside her heart and stay there. When his fingers explored her opening, she pushed back and he slowly inserted one inside. She sighed. Then he pulled it out and pushed in two fingers. Her pulse picked up speed. When he removed them, she held her breath until he added a third, stretching her. She backed toward him, wanting deeper penetration.

When he pulled his fingers out, she moaned. She didn't want to seem desperate, but she was.

Positioning his cock head at her entrance with one hand, he laid the other on her back. "You are tight, so let me go slow."

She nodded, not really hearing his words as every sense was focused on her tense core. He spread her labia and his cock just breached her opening.

He was wide and his head stretched her farther. Her excitement rose. *Finally.* She tightened around him, anxious to feel every inch.

Ware's voice came from her side. "Relax, Erin. He will be inside sooner if you allow him in. Let him pleasure you. You don't need to do anything."

Her body listened to Ware moments before her mind grasped what he said. She didn't have to work for this. All she had to do was enjoy, so opposite of her solitary habits.

Nase's cock slid in more and she relaxed more, allowing him to spread her as wide as he needed. Every nerve ending inside her jumped with pleasure, heating her from the inside out. The circular pressure on her shoulders that massaged and excited her had to be Ware again. How did he do that? Her curiosity dissipated as Nase pushed a little more. Being filled with his cock was like being completed. She craved this with her heart and soul.

"Are you ready for all of me, Fiya?"

"Yessss."

Nase's cock moved deeper, filling her, ramping up her heartbeat as little fireworks exploded inside her pussy until he hit her cervix.

He groaned, holding her hips tight against his pelvis. She took in deep breaths, trying to relax around him.

But then the pressure on her shoulders moved down her arms and traveled up to her breasts. It was as if someone brushed against them, back and forth, making her already hard nipples harder, and causing tension to build around Nase deep inside her.

He pressed himself against her inside wall, sending bolts of pleasure ricocheting through her body.

"You were made for me." He gripped her hips tighter. "I must make you mine."

His words caused her to shiver, the stark craving in his voice an aphrodisiac that made her juices flow.

He pulled back, and she almost cried out from the friction, but bit down hard for fear he'd stop. Slowly, he rocked forward until he had her hips tight against him again and another round of pleasure spread through her.

His next pullback was faster and he plunged inside her in one solid stroke. She cried out, unable to hold back as her pussy tensed around him, squeezing him for all she was worth.

Nase groaned as he forced his way back against her clinging sheath. "I can't control it." With his words his body slammed into hers and little stars filled her vision, her orgasm already starting. He speared her again and again and she shuddered as his battering flooded her senses with pure ecstasy.

When he finally came, the heat of his semen sent her orgasm spiraling throughout her body. She spun out of control as a scream tore from her throat. She shook with pleasure and gasped for air. When her world righted itself, she became aware of Nase hugging her around the waist.

She couldn't hold them up and collapsed onto the lounge. He rolled them to their sides, keeping his cock inside her as his rapid breaths brushed by her ear. She tried to relax, let her body come down from the excitement to enjoy the satisfaction she finally had.

Opening her eyes, she found Ware staring at her. Oh God, she'd never had a man watch her come, never mind watch her while having sex with his friend. It made her feel sexy. She pursed her lips and threw him a kiss.

His eyes widened before they turned predatory. Her heart skipped a beat at the possessiveness in his face, or maybe it was the red lighting. She lowered her gaze. They'd only just met. He was probably just turned on.

She glanced back at him, but he took another sip of water. Her gaze shifted to his lap and found his cock, hard and ready. She licked her lips, wanting to touch it, kiss it, lick it from base to tip. When she looked at his face again, his gaze was on her and this time it was clear he wanted her.

Nase licked behind her ear and she cringed. "Hey, that tickles." The tension between her legs moved to her shoulders.

"Really? And here I thought I was being sexy."

She turned her head to look at him and found him anything but disappointed. "How about you? Are you ticklish?"

He raised his brows in mock confusion. "Me? Ticklish? I think not."

Now that was a challenge if she ever heard one. Rolling away from him and disconnecting them, she reached forward to tickle him, but stopped at his look of horror.

"What is it?"

He stared at his penis. "That thing you put on. It's still there."

"You mean the condom?" She shook her head. How could they be so ignorant about protection? "Here, let me." Carefully, she pulled the condom off and dropped it in the small trash can just inside the sliding glass doors. "See? It caught all of your cum and protected you from mine, so there's no need for worry."

Nase stood, once again looking affronted. "I never was worried." He brushed past her and stalked into the suite.

She looked at Ware. "I guess you never have to guess where you stand with him."

He shook his head and the tiniest of smiles curled his lips. "No, you don't."

* * * * *

Erin stretched as the boat came to a stop. They must be docking for the day. Moving the curtains aside from where she lay on her bed, she turned her face to the sun as it filled their small cabin. Looking over at Craig's bunk, it was clear he'd been lucky with his lady last night.

She smiled. Not as lucky as she. For the first time she felt like a woman. Not just sexy, not simply experienced, but like a completely satisfied woman. Though Ware and Nase had wanted her to stay, she'd come back to her cabin last night. She'd sensed they planned no more sex and she had to wonder how Ware could stand it. It was best that she keep her own space. But they only allowed her to go if she promised to sleep naked. At first her sensitized body had stayed alert under the light cotton sheets, but eventually she'd been able to sleep.

A buzzing in her purse reminded her they must have cell coverage again. How many messages would she have this morning? Rising, she lifted her purse from the little table by the closet and checked her phone. Two messages from her mom, two messages from her boss and five messages from her little sister. Her mom probably looked for a shoulder to cry on as usual, and she just didn't have it in her to listen on such a beautiful morning. Maybe later. Her boss obviously still needed her and hadn't fired her if he'd left two messages, so she could always listen to those later and text him back, but her sister's calls concerned her.

Sitting back on the bed and crossing her bare legs, she dialed.

"Where have you been?" Trish's voice was a whole octave higher than usual.

"I told you, I'm on vacation, remember?"

"Oh yeah. But I didn't know you'd go somewhere without cell service."

"I'm on a cruise. There isn't cell service in all parts of the Caribbean Sea. What was so urgent that you called me five times in the last twelve hours?"

"I got a slash in my tire. They want forty dollars to put on a new one. My car is sitting in a parking lot and now the store says they're going to tow it if I don't move it by tonight."

Erin rubbed her thigh as she tried to guess what the real problem was. "Okay, so use your cash card at an ATM."

"I can't." Her sister sighed. "I overdrew my account last week and I don't get my unemployment check for another three days. I need your help."

Ah, now it became clear. "Did you talk to Mom?"

"Of course I talked to Mom. She's too busy with her own life to bother with me."

"Now, Trish, that isn't true. I'm sure—"

"Are you going to give me the cash or not?"

Erin uncrossed her legs and stood to stare out the window. "And how am I supposed to do that when I'm in the middle of the Caribbean Sea?" The pause on the other end made it clear her sister had completely forgotten where she was.

But that didn't stop her for long. "Do you have any cash in your condo? I still have a key from when you let me stay there for a couple weeks. I've been meaning to get it back to you, but I haven't seen you since last month."

Yeah, last month when Trish "borrowed" a hundred dollars. Her sister had stayed with her three months ago. Erin sighed. It wasn't as if her sister would suddenly figure out how to manage her own money. "Okay. I do have some cash in the cookie jar on the counter."

"The cookie jar? Really, sis?"

"Yeah, really. There's about eighty dollars in there. Take the forty you need and you can pay me back when you get paid at the end of the week. I'll be home on Sunday."

"I knew I could count on you. Thanks, Erin. You're my favorite sister."

"I'm your only—" The line went dead. Usually her sister's abrupt ways didn't bother her, but today they did. It was clear her sister took advantage of her, and Erin's patience with it grew thinner with every request.

Not ready to deal with whatever her boss might need from her as well, she put the phone away and rifled through her clothes. Today she would go ashore with the two hottest men on Earth, at least as far as she was concerned. Then maybe, just maybe they could have a lovely naked evening. She didn't mind being naked with them.

She grinned. As she passed the mirror on the way to the shower, she halted. Wait. She'd been naked since she woke up and hadn't even noticed. She'd never done that before. Maybe the ship's atmosphere had influenced her. Deep down she wanted to go naked in public just to please Ware and Nase, but she just didn't think she could. Then again, many things had changed for her this trip and she wouldn't count that out as a possibility.

Smiling wider, she jumped in the shower, anxious to start the day.

She was almost done when there was a knock on the bathroom door. "Hey, Erin. I need your help."

That phrase was getting on her nerves. She finished drying off and wrapped the towel around her before she stepped from the small room into the cabin.

Craig stood naked next to the window, impatiently waiting for her. His short blond hair and runner's build made him nothing to sneeze at, but compared to her two men, he was scrawny.

"What do you want, Craig?"

He turned and hesitated. "Did you do something with your hair?"

"No, I just have it up for my shower." She patted the bun at the back of her head.

He took a step closer. "You seem different."

She shrugged, moved over to her bed and sat. "So what is it?"

He flopped down on his bed. "I need you to come to a special cocktail party this evening."

"Why?"

"For the same reason I needed you to come on this cruise. It's for couples only. It will be on Deck Seven. Meet me at the central elevators down there at six."

"But what about dinner?"

"Oh there will be food there. Besides, the main buffet is open all night."

She had hoped to have dinner with Nase and Ware, not that they had asked her. There were really no plans past going ashore on St. Martin.

Craig dropped to his knees on the floor before her. "Please. They won't let me attend without my other half. It's just for a couple hours unless you want to stay longer. I just want to experience all that this lifestyle has to offer. Please say you will."

His puppy-dog eyes that had convinced her to come on the cruise in the first place didn't sway her now. "What about the blonde woman you slept with last night?"

He bowed his head. "I can't bring her. The reason I want to go to this party is that there is a woman who will be there and she indicated that if I came with you, she would consider having sex with me."

Erin looked at him shrewdly. Why did he have to bring her to have sex with another woman? Did this woman want her permission or something? "So I'm to play your pimp? This party doesn't include bondage and domination does it?"

His head snapped up. "No. Not tonight. Tonight is just a meet and greet. I promise."

She studied him. He may be telling the truth regarding the bondage, but he was hiding something. Guess she would learn more about Craig Mathews on this trip than she had ever contemplated knowing. "Okay. I'll be there."

"Whoohoo!" He jumped up, his penis flopping against his balls. "I owe you one."

"Yes, you do."

He grinned and kissed her on the cheek. "Are you sure you haven't done something different?"

Yeah, I got laid, dumbass. "Nope. Just the same old me."

"Right. Thanks, Erin. I'll see you at six."

Shaking her head, she dropped the towel as soon as the door closed and donned her bathing suit and sundress. A pair of flip-flops and a hat followed. Throwing suntan lotion, a towel and her sunglasses into her beach bag, she picked up her purse.

A warm tingle made its way across her skin and she grinned. Soon she'd be with her two gorgeous hunks again. She grabbed her phone and stilled. Did she really want that with her? What if there was an emergency and she needed to call 9-1-1 or whatever it was on this island? Ah hell, she wouldn't know what to call. Taking her wallet, she left the phone and shoved her purse in a drawer. She didn't want to know who else needed her. Today she just wanted to enjoy the company of her men.

✶ ✶ ✶ ✶ ✶

"This isn't good." Nase paced the length of the suite, his strides tense.

"It isn't bad either. You were able to satisfy yourself with Erin. Do you still think she is the one for us now that you've been inside her?" Ware raised his brow when Nase halted at his question.

"Of course I do. Now more than ever." He cracked his knuckles as he strode. "Her body is perfect. Did you notice the muscles in her thighs as I pumped into her? Her personality is precious and the woman is smart. Shit, Ware, we need to make her ours."

Ware sat at the table in the kitchen with his bowl of sugared cereal. What fascinated him had been Erin's eyes. A mix of colors normally, last night when she came they changed to green. He too wanted to make her eyes green with satisfaction but… "What about her ability, or lack thereof, to be nude? What about her willingness to live on another planet, in the jungle with no walled city to protect her?"

"First we have to tell her about Eden. How can she get used to the idea if she doesn't know it exists?"

"And when she doesn't believe us?" Ware took a spoonful of the cereal and sighed in pleasure. So much sugar on Earth would spoil him.

Nase stopped in front of the table. "We show her."

Ware stopped chewing.

Nase nodded. "Yes. We open the portal and show her. She will have to step through eventually anyway if we are to take her back, and we can't go slowly. We only have five more days on this ship and then we have to return."

Swallowing, Ware ran through the pros and cons of Nase's suggestion. Convincing Erin that they came from another planet would be hard. Making her comfortable with her own nudity could be just as difficult. Naralina was indeed a naked city and the men he and Nase led were from there. To have a beloved that was not nude would pose serious issues. Starting the bond with her should be fairly easy if they could figure out a way around cock wrappers. Completing it would be up to her.

Nase was right, they didn't have much time. They would have to tell her only what she needed to know and fill her in on the rest once she was on Eden. He wasn't completely comfortable with that solution, but it was their only option unless they wanted to risk using the portal multiple months in a row, but that could put everyone at risk. He hated keeping information from her, but time was their enemy, and leaving her for even one month would be hard to stomach. "Okay."

"Really?"

He looked up at Nase. "Yes. We need to get her comfortable with her own nudity in public, convince her we come from Eden, begin the bond with her and then take her home by Sunday. We have few choices."

Instead of the wide smile Nase usually made when he got his way, he frowned.

Ware scooped another spoonful of cereal into his mouth, but the sweet pleasure dulled at the challenge before them. They had no choice.

CHAPTER FIVE

Erin couldn't help the big smile on her face as she strolled between Nase and Ware down the narrow path to the beach. What woman could blame her? She had two gorgeous hunks and they would soon be sunning on a beach. She'd be the envy of every woman there.

For such a popular place, she was surprised by how small the path was. She'd heard more than a couple of groups disembarking the ship talking about Orient Beach. Then again, it was a nude beach so maybe it had to be tucked away.

The salty smell of the ocean caught her just before the path opened up to a small beach flanked by two coral rock heads. Between them was two hundred feet of pure, white sand and the beautiful turquoise water she had seen from the ship. Now this was a beach, except it was empty.

Ware stepped up to her, his body barely touching hers. "Do you like it?"

She tilted her head up to look at him and caught her breath. His presence was almost overpowering. Her body reacted to him like a candle lit by a match, slowly melting but hot. Staring into his green gaze was mesmerizing.

The slightest twitching at the corner of his mouth had her mind taking over again. "I love it. But where are all the people?"

"It's just us. Everyone else is probably on Orient Beach, which I imagine is quite crowded by now. We thought you might like to try a more secluded spot."

She turned her body toward his. "Try it for what?"

"For being nude."

She stepped back. "Why?"

He cocked his head slightly. "Why not? Did you sleep naked last night?"

She flushed. "Yes."

Ware closed the space between them, pressing his hard body against her and cupping her cheek. "Then I would ask that you spend your time on this beach with us naked."

Oh God, when he used that tone of voice she craved to do whatever he wanted. Again she wondered if he was a hypnotist.

She looked around the secluded beach. They were surrounded by hills and the only house she could see was far up on a mountain. "Okay. But you have to put lotion on my back. I don't want to burn."

Ware smiled, as in a real smile, and her heart jumped into double time, causing her to catch a breath. A warmth filled her chest as if she belonged. She clasped his hand against her cheek and shuddered at the sensual feelings that coursed through her body like a wave.

He pulled back. "I would be happy to help you."

Erin shivered at the vision of Ware rubbing lotion onto her back.

Nase ran up to them, already naked. "The water feels like home. Anyone interested in swimming?"

She grinned. "I am. Skinny dipping I've done. Though it was at night." She winked at Ware. "Where should we set our towels?"

Ware took her bag from her. "You go swim. I'll set up."

"Okay." She quickly pulled off her sundress, throwing it over his arm. Taking one more glance around the secluded spot, she untied her rainbow-striped string bikini, and dropped the top into her bag. Before she could lose her nerve, she pulled down her bottoms and they followed her top.

Ware nodded in approval, but Nase grabbed her hand. "Come on, let's catch some waves."

He pulled her to the water's edge, but there were no waves to catch. Without hesitation, he scooped her up and walked into the water until he was chest deep. "I've waited so long to hold you."

She wrapped her arms around his neck. "I'm so glad you came on this cruise. I've never met anyone like you and Ware."

He laughed. "I'm not so unique, but Ware is definitely one of a kind."

"You really care about him."

"Of course. Like I care about you. I don't know what he ever saw in me, but he chose me as his friend and for that I will be forever grateful."

He cared about her. That phrase hit deep, forcing her to look at Nase with new appreciation. "Why wouldn't Ware want you as a friend? You are strong, intelligent, honest, fearless."

"Now how would you know that?"

She shrugged. "I just do."

He grinned. "Wild nights! Wild nights! Were I with thee, Wild nights should be Our luxury!"

She froze. "That's Emily Dickinson."

"Of course."

She shook her head. "Let me down."

He let her legs fall to the soft sand beneath the water, but he held on to her hand. "Erin, what's wrong?"

"Nothing, nothing is wrong. It's just *that* poem. That poem is very special to me."

Nase grasped her shoulder and his face turned serious, something she hadn't witnessed before. "Why is it special, Erin?"

She couldn't look at him. He was so honest, he made her want to tell him the truth, but she couldn't. She couldn't tell anyone about the day she'd found the handwritten poem by the author herself. She'd been seventeen and already in love with Emily Dickinson's poetry. When she'd crawled over the ropes at the Dickinson homestead to touch the pillow of the poet she'd enjoyed so much, she'd noticed the slip of paper peeking out from beneath the pillow. Too curious to ignore it, she pulled the paper out to find the poem *Wild Nights! Wild Nights!* She didn't even have time to read it before she heard people approaching. Stuffing it into the pocket of her jeans, she scrambled out of there. She didn't read it entirely until she was home.

That's when she realized the enormity of what she'd done. It was in the author's own hand with scratch-outs and ink blots. She could go to jail. "No one has ever quoted those lines or mentioned that poem to me. In school we read all her death poetry and they said she was a recluse. It wasn't until college that I actually found that poem in a complete book of her poetry."

Nase pulled her toward him, the warm water lapping around them. "It's a special poem to me. And I mean those lines. With the three of us together, like last night, wild nights should be our luxury…forever."

Before she could answer, Nase's lips were on hers. She tried to force the poem from her mind, but Nase's words finally made the meaning clear. He nudged her mouth open and delved inside with his tongue. He tasted of berry jelly, like the kind found in jelly donuts, her favorite flavor, and she concentrated fully on the heat building between them. As she wrapped her arms around his neck, he pulled her tighter against him, his hard cock pressing into her abdomen. He buried his hand in her hair as he tilted her head.

As he righted her, he licked at her lips, pressing kisses along the outside. "Erin."

The single word, the kiss, his seriousness finally penetrated her brain. He'd said "forever." He didn't just care for her. He loved her. She was loved. For the first time, true joy filled her soul.

Wait. She pulled away and his lips traveled down her neck. She hadn't known him long but even Ware had agreed that Nase hid nothing, but he hid his love now. Why?

"Nase?"

"Hmm."

"I'd like to return to the beach."

He stopped his nibbles on her shoulder and looked at her. "Is something wrong?"

She shook her head. "Nothing except I'm turning into a prune." She lifted her hands to show him her fingers, which were indeed becoming quite wrinkled from the water. But she really wanted to talk to Ware. Did he know Nase had fallen for her so quickly?

He lifted her hand to his lips and kissed it, his tongue snaking out to lap her palm.

She squealed.

He grinned. "I'll race you back in."

She didn't answer, too caught up in the fun of the moment. She plunged in and swam for shore, determined to beat him, but he didn't play fair. He grabbed her ankle and pulled her back, stroking her thigh. She laughed as she wriggled away again and he pushed through the water ahead of her.

Two could play that game. She grabbed his ankle with both hands and yanked hard. His head went under and she ran her hand up to grab his cock.

He sputtered as his head cleared the surface again and his hands came up. "I surrender. Do what you will."

She smiled. "I don't think so. That's exactly what you wanted. Nice try." With that, she ran through the shallows toward the beach. When she made it onto dry sand first, she jumped up. "I win!" As she came down she froze.

Standing on the beach next to Ware was an older couple. Both were naked and both smiled at her. She spun around, too embarrassed to look at them.

She heard Nase's breathing a half second before he scooped her up and carried her forward. She turned her head into his shoulder. "Stop. I can't go over there."

He halted. "Why?"

"Because there are other people here."

"That's right. So?"

Frustrated, she glared up at him. "I'm naked."

His gaze was sympathetic, if not understanding. "Erin, we all are. If you had clothes on then you could feel embarrassed." He walked forward with her in his arms.

Her body flushed with embarrassment as they drew closer. When they were within hearing, he put her feet down and took her hand. "Come, let's go meet them."

She pulled back, but he would have none of it.

Ware nodded as they approached. "Nase, Erin, I'd like you to meet Margaret and Henry."

The older woman's smile was wide. "Oh, call me Mimi. Everyone else does and it makes me feel as if I'm as young as you."

Nase wiggled his eyebrows. "Mimi it is and young you look too."

"Oh now don't be silly."

Erin relaxed as the older woman blushed. She had to be in her seventies at least, but was rather lean and fit. Nase's kindness made her proud of him, which didn't make any sense.

"Nice to meet you, son." Henry held out his hand and Nase shook. Erin smiled. The older man smiled back. He didn't ogle her breasts or try to look at her pussy.

Mimi hooked her arm around Henry. "We have been coming to this little beach for over twenty years. We never know who we will meet."

Erin couldn't resist. "You've been a nudist for that long?"

"Yes. Unfortunately it wasn't longer, but my first husband, God rest his soul, and I never knew this lifestyle existed." She squeezed Henry's arm. "I'm just so lucky I met Henry."

Erin looked at Nase. "I know the feeling."

Mimi's eyebrows raised and she let go of Henry's arm to step up to Erin. "I feel a story in those words. Let's go sit over there in the shade to protect your white skin and have us a little girl talk."

Before she could say a word, Erin found her arm linked with Mimi's as she was propelled away. She looked over her shoulder to see Nase grinning and Ware nodding. Returning her attention to her new companion, she was once again impressed at how comfortable the woman was being nude. "I think you need to tell me how you met Henry first. I'm just dying to hear."

Mimi brightened as she steered them toward a rock with a towel draped over it. "Honey, it was one of those happenings that you could never have imagined, but afterward you are so very thankful for."

Erin nodded. She understood that. Meeting Nase and Ware had been sheer luck. Did that mean that she might be with them twenty years from now like Mimi and Henry?

An unexpected tide of hope filled her and she pressed her hand to her chest in surprise. Could it be?

* * * * *

Erin stood at the center elevator bank of the seventh deck at exactly 6:00 p.m., but Craig was nowhere to be seen. She'd give him fifteen minutes. She kicked herself a dozen times for agreeing to help him with this party. It was last thing she would do for him. After spending a lovely day with Mimi, Henry, Ware and Nase, and feeling more comfortable being nude, she was disappointed she couldn't go when her men asked her to dinner. They understood, of course, that she had already agreed to another engagement, but the more time she spent with them, the more she wanted to be with them, and every minute away bothered her. Too bad she didn't have a clone who could go to the party for her.

She smoothed the lavender ombre dress she wore. It reminded her of one of Deanna Troi's dresses in *Star Trek Next Generation* Season 1, but had a flair skirt and she'd been sure to wear nothing underneath. She sincerely hoped her men would like it.

The elevator doors opened and Craig stepped out, naked.

"You're late."

He stopped. "I'm sorry. I didn't know we were in a rush."

"Actually, I am. I have other people to be with."

Craig winked. "Oh, I think you are going to like these people too."

She rolled her eyes. "If you say so."

He stared at her for a moment. "Is everything okay? You seem different."

"Let's go to this party. I'm going to need some food or my low blood sugar will turn me into a wicked witch."

"I get that. This way."

They wended their way along the narrow hallway toward the front of the ship. This is where Nase and Ware had their suite only on a higher level. Craig stopped at a door at the bow and knocked. When it opened, they walked into a larger gathering room, obviously set up for just such a party.

An older man in great shape, with just a bit of gray at his temples approached them "Welcome. I'm Adam and I'm your host for this evening's party. We're so glad you could join us."

Erin smiled. The man was very laid-back. She liked that. "We? Where's your other half?" She hated to admit it, but she didn't fully trust Craig's story.

"I'm right here." Another man stepped around them. He was a little taller than Adam and had long white hair pulled back in a ponytail. "I'm Len, Adam's husband. You must be Erin and Craig."

Craig shook hands. "Brandy invited us."

Len stiffened. "Really?"

"Yeah, is she here?" Craig scanned the room. He obviously had a one-track mind.

Erin shook her head at the other men. "Craig, why don't you go look for her?"

"Good idea." Within seconds, he was out of hearing.

"I'm sorry. This is our first nude cruise and he is a bit excited." She smiled apologetically.

Adam hooked her arm in his. "Don't worry. We'll introduce you."

The two men were the perfect hosts and she soon forgot about Craig. She was actually enjoying herself. The people were very nice. Some were completely nude, but others had on sexy outfits, or what she suspected they thought was sexy. Then again, they may have worn them to be funny like the man with the tuxedo bib under his penis. Another man wore a netted Speedo that was definitely sexy. What would Nase look like in that? The women were dressed more elaborately with feathers, see-through materials, and even leather straps. But in this crowd, she wasn't the least bit uncomfortable in her lavender one-shoulder dress with the short, flowing skirt. However, she had the uneasy feeling that later in the night, the party would become a bit too wild for her comfort.

The waiters were the only ones completely dressed, and they wandered the room, offering wine and munchies. Erin snagged a bacon-wrapped scallop as it passed by and popped it in her mouth.

Craig grabbed her arm just as she swallowed. "Come on. I want you to meet Brandy."

After excusing herself, she shook off the concerned look Adam gave her and followed Craig through the crowd, managing to snatch another bite, this one a deep-fried mushroom with a spicy Russian dressing. Craig stopped before a tall woman with long red hair, though Erin wasn't sure the woman was really tall as she had on platform heels that had to be at least six inches high. With her were two men, one blond and one platinum. Both had shaved all the hair from their bodies, which made her itch just thinking about that trying to grow back.

"Erin, I'd like you to meet Brandy."

Brandy nodded regally. "It's nice to meet you. I've seen a lot of Craig, but nothing of you." Her look was practically predatory as she scanned Erin's dress and said the word "nothing."

Erin pasted on a smile. "I know, but we have different interests, so you won't see me clinging to his every move."

Craig swallowed hard as the two men grinned. Brandy turned toward them. "Then let me introduce you to Leo and Ice."

Leo and Ice? Really? As the men shook hands with her, it became clear that Brandy was part of a threesome, but would probably be just as open to an orgy. Good for her, but that wasn't Erin's cup of tea.

In no time Craig monopolized Brandy and the two men were chatting her up. She managed to snag a glass of wine and another scallop wrapped in bacon, but she was seriously hungry. Though she dropped a few hints about food, neither man picked up on it. Okay, if there was one thing Nase had taught her, it was to be blunt. "So where's the kitchen?"

The men looked at each other. Ice raised a platinum brow. "It's back here."

She looked around the corner and found a narrow hallway with an open door. She would have hesitated except she caught the scent of cooked onions. That had to be in something more substantial.

Leo sidled up next to her in his jaguar thong. "I love kitchens."

She ignored him and moved down the hallway, her hunger leading her along one track only—food. Inside the small room she found a whole tray of pigs in a blanket and promptly stuffed one in her mouth.

Leo and Ice came in and shut the door.

She looked up. "I'm sorry, I'm really hungry. Would you like some?"

The two men moved to each side of her, pushing the tray away. Ice licked her shoulder. "We'd love some."

"What?" She stepped aside quickly. "No, not of me. I meant the food." She pointed at the tray.

Leo stalked her, blocking her exit. "You don't have to play shy with us. We know you like men and the more the better."

CHAPTER SIX

Erin tried to think over the alarm bells going off in her head. Had they seen her with Nase and Ware? She needed to stay calm. "That may be true, but I already have mine."

The men looked at each other in confusion until Ice replied, "Right. Us."

They caught her between them. From behind, Leo grabbed her hands and pulled them above her as Ice pressed his cock in its see-through Speedo against her belly.

She struggled to pull her hands down. "Dammit, I said no." She brought her knee up to catch Ice in the balls, when the door to the kitchen flew open.

Nase grabbed Ice by the neck and pushed him up the wall while Ware pulled her into his arms. Leo made a run for the door, but Ware looked at him and Leo's head snapped to the side before he crumpled to the floor, moaning.

Her heart beat so fast she was dizzy.

Ware whispered in her ear, calming her. "You're safe now. No one will hurt you. You're safe."

A gurgling sound penetrated her adrenaline haze. She lifted her head from Ware's chest to see Ice's face turning bright red. "Nase." Her voice was ragged. She pushed it for more volume. "Nase, don't kill him."

"Why not?" The feral growl that came from him made her shiver.

"I don't want to see you in prison. He's not worth it."

She only received another growl in response, but he did lower the man, though he kept his hand around Ice's throat. He spoke through gritted teeth. "What were you doing?"

Ice opened his mouth but no words came out.

Ware rubbed her back, holding her tight to him. "Loosen up a bit, Nase, so he can speak."

She watched as Ice worked to swallow around Nase's hand. "We were just looking to have some fun." The hand around the man's throat tightened.

"Nase." Ware's stern voice must have helped Nase find some control.

"And when she said she didn't want to?"

Ice swallowed again. "Her boyfriend there said she liked to play shy and was into force. We thought it was all part of her kink."

Nase let go of the man's throat and sent his fist into the wall.

Ice crumpled to the floor in a faint.

Ware turned her head to look at him. "Are you okay?"

She nodded. "Yes, I just want to get out of here."

"Nase, let's go."

She took two steps, but her shaking returned and her knees gave way. Ware scooped her up and squeezed down the narrow hall. When they reached the main room, everyone stared.

She scanned the room for Craig, but he was nowhere in sight and neither was Brandy. That didn't take long. She'd obviously been used…again.

Ware and Nase strode through the room without a word. As they approached the door to the hall, Adam stepped before them. "I apologize if any in our group behaved poorly."

Nase stepped in front of them. "Poorly? They were going to, going to…" He turned and looked at her, shaking with rage. He whipped his head around. "They were going to force her against her will."

Adam's gasp was echoed by all those behind them. "That is not our way. They will be banned. That is not tolerated here."

Erin noticed Nase fisting his hands, barely controlling himself.

Ware tightened his hold on her. "We will be leaving now."

"Of course." Adam stumbled to the side as if unexpectedly pushed.

Nase pulled open the door and strode through.

When they entered the elevator, Ware let her feet down. "Nase. Hold Erin please."

The man had been staring at the closed elevator doors, but at Ware's voice he turned around. Erin wasn't sure who needed comfort more, but as he wrapped her in his arms, she didn't care. He buried his face in her hair. "Never again. Never, I promise."

She pressed her cheek against his shoulder, her tears of relief wetting his skin.

When the elevator stopped, Ware ushered them down the hall. "Open the door, Erin."

She looked up to find they were at her room. The room she shared with Craig. Craig who "needed" her for all his own selfish reasons. Craig who threw her under the bus in thanks. Fumbling for her key, she shook with anger, but managed to dig it out from her dress pocket. Ware took it from her and opened the door.

She stepped inside, wanting more than anything to find Craig there, but he wasn't. He was with Brandy somewhere having sex, the true reason he'd come on the cruise. The very reason the organizers insisted on couples and not men like him.

She walked to her bed and sat. Ware joined her, taking her hand in his large one, but Nase stayed in the doorway, his rage still palpable.

"Erin, you have to pack." Ware rubbed the back of her hand with his thumb.

"Huh?"

"You are staying in our suite for the rest of the cruise. If you want, you can even have your own bedroom, but you will no longer be staying in this cabin."

He didn't have to say the words "with Craig." He was right. She needed to vacate. If he and Nase hadn't come into that kitchen when they did…wait. "How did you know where to find me?"

"You can thank Nase and his impatience for that."

Nase harrumphed, but didn't elaborate.

Ware squeezed her hand, bringing her attention back to him. "You told us you had a 6:00 p.m. cocktail party and Nase didn't want to wait longer than we had to, so he suggested waiting nearby until you were done. But when we reviewed the activities for the day, the only cocktail party at that time was on Deck Seven. That's when we knew we had to find you immediately."

She crinkled her nose. "What did the deck number have to do with finding me right away?"

Ware glanced at Nase. She looked at him too to see the vein in his neck pulsing hard, his crossed forearms tighter than muscles should ever be. His rage had escalated.

She turned back to Ware and raised her eye brow expectantly.

"Deck Seven is the swingers deck."

"The swingers, the swingers…" She stood as blood shot through her veins. "That lousy, good-for-nothing bastard! If I ever see him again, I'm going to twist his balls up over his head and light them on fire." She fisted and unfisted her hands, feeling as if she couldn't get enough air.

Ware laid his hand on her arm and she glanced down at him. The corner of his mouth had turned up.

She turned on him. "Are you laughing at me?"

"No, I'm proud of you."

That pacified her a bit, but she still wanted to take her anger out on Craig. Maybe if she wished really hard he would come to their cabin right now. She looked at the door as if willing him to walk in. After a few minutes of silence, she let out her breath.

Nase unfolded his arms. "How about you pack a few things and we go to our suite and make love. We can come back here tomorrow for the rest of your belongings."

At his words, her body came to attention. She clung to Nase's words "make love." She wanted them both against her, to erase the evening's fiasco. "Yes. I'll just grab a couple items from the bathroom."

In a few minutes she had her beach bag stuffed with some clothes and a few toiletries. Without a backward glance, she accompanied her men to their suite.

* * * * *

Nase watched the steaming water fill the large round bathtub in their suite. Prepping the room for Erin had been his excuse to step away from her, to regroup, find some control. He'd never experienced such white-hot rage before. Seeing the two men on her broke what control he had. He was aware of his potential for violence, always holding it in check, even when attacked, but tonight he'd stepped over the edge. If Ware's calming presence hadn't been there…

He dunked his hand in the filling tub and adjusted the temperature with more cold water. It had to be just right for her. He'd fallen hard for Erin and what he planned to do he couldn't share with Ware. Ware would tell him it wasn't right, but he didn't care about right anymore. He cared about Erin and that was right. He had to make her his, and if he did so then Ware would be forced to follow, but to do that he had to have her so ready for penetration she would forget about the cock wrappers she'd brought with her. He loved her and the only way he could protect her was if they bonded.

He turned off the water and pulled extra towels from the cabinet. He would never break Dickinson Law. It had brought civilization back to Eden. He respected it too much, but he had spoken the truth to Ware. He wasn't above a little seduction and tonight was the night. Stepping out into the main room, he expected Erin to be cuddled up with Ware, but that was not the case and he sucked in his breath.

She was bent over, completely naked, to reach something in the bottom of the refrigerator. Ware sat at the table, appreciating the view. Shit, the man must have the will of the Crius to resist that ass, though he doubted those aliens had ever seen anything that tempting. "Your bath is ready."

Her head popped up and she took a popsicle from her mouth. "Thank you."

He stared, all his blood rushing to his cock. Her mouth around him suddenly seemed imperative. He glanced at Ware, who watched him, the corner of his mouth quirking.

"Ah shit!" Stepping to the counter, he ignored Erin's puzzled look, and grabbed the plate of brownies. "I'll be on the balcony."

"Is Nase okay?" Erin's concerned look for Nase crept into Ware's heart.

Nase was right. She would be their perfect agapayto. It was time to make her theirs. "He's fine. You are such a temptation that he had to take a moment to himself."

She leaned against the counter and pondered that as she sucked on the popsicle, her lips turning a light blue from the chemicals in the icy dessert. "It's so hard to believe that. You have to understand, for years no men wanted me in that way, though I have lots of male friends. Only my very first boyfriend was interested in me beyond friendship and well, it just seems like since I came on this cruise I suddenly have too many men attracted to me. Who knew a nude cruise could do that?"

First boyfriend? That couldn't be? "Erin, how old were you when you had this first boyfriend?"

She took another suck on the popsicle, almost to the bottom now, providing an image of what it would be like for her to suck on him right to his balls. Like Nase, he found himself grasping for control, but his upbringing put the woman above all else, especially this woman.

She wouldn't meet his gaze. "I was a little young, only sixteen when I had my first lover. It was strange, as we were only together for four months and then he lost interest." Her brows puckered in puzzlement.

Ware fisted his hands beneath the table. They had been too late. They blocked her pheromones to keep her pure, not knowing she'd already been broken. It wouldn't affect their bonding, but it had been important to Nase that they be her first. Ware looked out to the balcony where his friend paced. Would he care? The answer was obvious. No.

She was theirs and he would tell Nase tonight they would start the bond. It wouldn't be complete until they brought her home, which would be her choice. He still had doubts about her safety if she came to Eden, but he couldn't give her up. She'd always been his hope for a future, but now…now she was his life.

Erin walked to the trash and dropped the wooden stick of her popsicle into it. "I think I'm ready for that bath now." She stepped toward him, comfortable in her nakedness around them. A good sign.

"Thank you for coming to my rescue." She bent and gave him a featherlight kiss on his lips, but when she would have stood again, he snaked his hand around her neck and held her close. He licked at her lips and at her intake of breath, gently pushed his tongue inside her mouth. She tasted sweet and cold and his cock hardened. He never could resist sweet. He stroked her tongue with his before sucking it into his mouth. Removing his hand from her neck, he withdrew and separated them.

She remained where she was, her eyes closed. Finally, her eyelids fluttered open. "Ware?"

He raised a brow. "Yes?"

"Nothing. I'm going to get clean now. I'd really like to wash the touch of Leo and Ice off my skin."

He nodded and watched her disappear into their bathroom. The cool anger of the evening's event rose inside his heart, but it wasn't directed at the men she mentioned. Rather it was her roommate, Craig, who would feel his wrath. Nase would simply kill him, but Ware already had other ideas that would make the man's suffering last much longer.

Rising, he smiled inside at the hard-on he sported. No matter how angry or upset he was, no matter the control he exercised, his cock would always reveal his desire for Erin. Striding to the sliding glass door, he caught Nase's attention.

His friend stepped inside. "I see she got to you too."

Ware ignored the statement and looked at the half-eaten plate of brownies. "Feeling better?"

Nase shrugged. "Some. I won't feel better until we make her ours."

"Tonight."

"Really?" Nase grabbed his arm. "You agree?"

"Yes. She is ours. I will join her to help her wash, then bring her to your room and we will bond to her."

"But we can't tell her yet. She'll have no idea that she's ours."

Ware tensed at Nase's frown. He didn't like keeping important information from Erin either, but he pacified himself with the fact that they would tell her soon, as soon as she agreed to come to Eden with them. Besides, the bonding wouldn't finalize until she arrived on their planet. It would still be her choice. For him, there was no other choice. "No, she won't, she isn't ready yet to consider forever with us, but we will tell her soon, let her decide if she wishes to complete it."

"What about her cock wrappers?"

In order for them to bond to her, they both had to come inside her consecutively, bringing her to climax both times. It was critical their semen mix within her. "If she asks for one, we will have to concede. If that is the case, then we will try again tomorrow, but if we are deserving of her, she will be too distracted to remember those."

Nase's grin lit his face as he squeezed Ware's arm once more before letting go. "I'll be ready."

Ware raised a brow. "I don't doubt that."

Nase's laugh put Ware in a better mood, as usual. His friend's emotions kept him grounded. Would Erin's as well? He wouldn't know until they brought her home, but the possibilities for his life from tonight forward had his spirit expanding.

CHAPTER SEVEN

Ware turned and headed for the bathroom, stopping in the kitchen to grab a large plastic cup. Opening the door, he stepped inside.

Erin lay like a water nymph of ancient times, her legs crossed at the ankles and propped on the edge of the oblong tub. Her head rested on the back with her pale hair thrown over the side. The water floated her breasts, her nipples not quite breaking the surface. He was provided a perfect view of her curvy hips and the small triangle of hair at the juncture of her legs.

He lowered his voice to its most soothing. "Would you like me to wash your hair?"

She opened her eyes and her gaze swept him from head to toe, causing each place she viewed to tense. "Okay."

What he wanted was her assent to come home with him, but he satisfied himself that he could do this small chore for her now. Picking up the shampoo, he knelt and set it on the floor. "Sit up."

She did as he requested, bringing her beautiful breasts above the surface, droplets falling from her nipples into the water below.

He swallowed hard. Using the cup he'd brought, he scooped water into it. "Tilt your head back."

As she did, he sluiced water over her hair, turning it a deep honey. After a few more cups, he lathered her soft strands, gently rubbing her scalp.

"Oh Ware, I've never had anyone do this for me. This is heavenly."

Such a small task and yet so appreciated. He wondered at her life until now. Yes, they had checked on her regularly, but they didn't know enough about her, about how she dealt with challenges or celebrated successes. There was so much to learn about her. Another task he would thoroughly enjoy.

When he finished massaging her scalp, he picked up the cup and rinsed her hair with fresh warm water.

As he finished, she opened her eyes and looked at him. "That was the nicest thing anyone has ever done for me."

A lump formed in his throat and he coughed. "I would do so much more for you, if you allow it."

She tilted her head, holding his gaze. "I believe you."

"Good. Now if you wish, I can help you wash."

Ware caught his breath as Erin smiled, a beautiful, open look that said she loved being with them. "I think I'll do that myself as it will go a lot faster and I am anxious to enjoy more time with both of you."

"As you wish." Standing, he stepped back from the tub and leaned against the far wall.

Erin's eyes grew round. "Are you going to watch me?"

"Yes."

The flush that stained her cheeks was so becoming he almost wished she'd never lose her modesty, but she needed to be comfortable being nude in all situations if she was to adapt to Eden and be his and Nase's agapayto.

Luckily, she didn't ask him to leave or he would have done as she wished. Instead she slowly rose, her skin glistening as the water sluiced down her body. He sucked in his breath to retain control, but his cock rose. Quickly, she lathered the soap over her body, not looking at him, but the view of her in profile was plenty. Her nipples became hard despite her fast attentions to them, and his gaze remained on her ass after she had soaped it clean. He couldn't help watching the small clusters of bubbles slowly slide over her curved cheeks.

In little time, she had unplugged the drain and turned on the rain-head shower. Ware crossed his arms to keep himself in check. The water washed the soap suds down her curves, and he watched them disappear past her defined calves. When the water shut off, he moved his gaze upward until he met hers.

"Can you hand me a towel?"

He shook his head. "Step out. I want to dry you."

"Okay." Her cautious voice had him chuckling inside. If she wondered at him drying her, how would she react when they told her about Eden? His only hope on that score was her lifetime interest in science fiction. He lowered his brows. At least he hoped it had been a lifetime interest.

"Ware?"

He looked her in the eyes briefly, happy to be reminded of his task, then dropped his gaze to her toes. Slowly, he air-touched her, moving the air against her feet to push the water droplets off. Inch by inch he raised his gaze and his stream of air up her legs. As he dried the triangle of hair that hid her sweet woman's sheath, he resisted the urge to ask her to spread her legs. If he stroked her there, he wouldn't be able to control himself in the bonding.

Instead he shifted his gaze farther up her body, watching her stomach go concave as she sucked in her breath. When he reached her breasts she shivered. "Are you cold?"

Her voice trembled slightly as she spoke. "No. Actually, I'm hot."

He bit down on the grin that wanted to appear and added a bit of pressure against her nipples, already hard from his touch, but he enjoyed the vision of her pebbled areolas. As he made his way up her neck, he lightened the push of air. "Close your eyes."

This time he did grin, pleased with how quick she was to obey. When he reached her hair he stopped. "Turn around."

She did as he asked and he slowly pushed the water from her body. When he finished, he uncrossed his arms and picked up a towel. "Here. You can dry your hair with this. It will take far too long for me to do it and we both know Nase is not that patient."

As she took the towel, she studied him. "You know, you are going to have to show me how you do that before this cruise is over. That is a trick that I just have to learn." She bent over and threw the towel around her hair, twisting it. She stood and tucked it into itself somehow.

"What if I told you it wasn't a trick, but a special power I have?"

"I would be thrilled but disappointed because that would mean I can't learn it." She gave him a cocky smile. "But we both know it's a trick. As much as I sigh over super powers and alien worlds, even I know there are no such things." With that remark she sauntered out of the room, her naked ass teasing him.

He waited a moment. "It's not a trick." When he had himself under control enough to complete the bonding, he left, and made for Nase's bedroom.

* * * * *

Erin sprawled on the king-size bed. "This is huge. I didn't know they offered suites with beds this big on a cruise ship. Guess I should have investigated this whole trip more before coming on board." At her statement, she couldn't help tensing at the reason she was even on the ship in the first place—Craig. But then she looked at the two males standing at the foot of the bed and couldn't stay mad. "Of course, if I had done that, I never would have come and I'm very glad I did." She gave them what she hoped was a come-hither look. Nase answered with a devilish grin of his own, but Ware simply raised a brow.

They were two amazingly attractive men with muscles in all the right places. Whether she gazed at Nase's biceps or Ware's pectorals, Nase's quads or Ware's glutes, it didn't matter. They had her salivating from here until Tuesday, as her neighbor used to say. And right now she wanted some of the hard cock these two men sported. "Okay, here's the deal."

Ware immediately frowned and Nase tensed. They really needed to chill. She stretched her arms over her head, though her legs remained crossed. "You two can do anything you like to me as long as I get to suck on one of your cocks."

Nase relaxed, but Ware looked at her shrewdly. "Anything?"

A stab of excitement hit her belly at his expression. He truly meant that she allow them anything. She squinted as she contemplated. Did she dare? No, that was the wrong question. Did she trust these two to take care of her and not harm her? She did. Though she'd only known them a couple days, she trusted them. They had looked out for her since the minute they met.

She propped herself up on her elbows. "Yes, anything. Deal?"

The men looked at each other, all playing gone. The seriousness as they nodded to each other had her curious. It was just sex.

Ware met her gaze, his face serious. "Yes, you have a deal."

Why did she suddenly feel as if she'd said something wrong? She was about to suggest they forget it when she noticed Ware's lips forming the most seductive grin she'd ever seen. Her breath caught in her throat and she was suddenly thankful he didn't reveal that look on a regular basis. Moving her arms out from under her, she dropped back into the soft sheets, which helped her breathe. "So whose cock do I get to lick and suck and nip at?"

Ware shook his head. "You are playing with fire, Bedia."

"I hope so. Is that another endearment?"

Ware moved around the side of the bed. "Yes, it is. For only someone dear would be given to both of us as we will take you tonight."

A thrill of unknown expectations had her pussy moistening already. She could probably come just listening to them, but she wouldn't let them know that. Instead, she licked her lips in anticipation of the blowjob she wanted to give.

Ware moved onto the bed. "Put your hands down by your sides."

"Okay, but you know I will need them to hold you." She liked that Ware's jaw tightened, an obvious sign that she had his interest. Sometimes he could be as expressionless as a Cylon and seeing him react had her grinning.

Carefully, he straddled her shoulders, his thigh muscles taut on either side of her biceps. Though she couldn't grasp his cock with her hands, she had to admit it put him in the perfect position for her to enjoy. The only problem was, he was completely in control. Bending her elbows, she grasped his tight ass.

Air whistled through his teeth and his cock jerked. So maybe the position did have some advantages. Ware lifted his cock from close to her lips and moved his hips forward, presenting her with his balls. Hmm, so he wanted to go slow. She was fine with that.

She had just begun to lick when Nase's hands ran up the insides of her legs and pushed them wider. She couldn't see anything he did because Ware blocked her view. Anticipation shot through her like static electricity and her juices truly flowed. Did Nase notice?

Wanting to show her appreciation, she sucked one of Ware's balls into her mouth and rolled it with her tongue. His increased breaths made it clear he enjoyed what she did. Carefully, and not without a few misses, she caught his other ball and sucked it inside as well, gently keeping them inside, closing her lips.

Ware's low moan was echoed by her own as she felt the first lap of Nase's tongue on her pussy.

He was more vocal than Ware. "Ah, you taste so good, Fiya."

She hummed her agreement, vibrating Ware's sac. He pulled away.

She released him and winked. "That was just an appetizer. I'm ready for my main meal now."

Ware held his cock before her and brushed her lips with its head. She darted out her tongue now and again to taste him. He was warm and sweet-smelling, that banana-like scent rising from his skin. Just as he pushed the head of his wide cock into her mouth, Nase pushed his tongue inside her. She groaned, a sound that was echoed by the men.

Nase's fingers pulled her folds apart and explored every inch, darting inside on regular intervals. She found herself making similar actions with her tongue on Ware's cock. She laved its head, but sucked hard every time Nase plunged his tongue inside her.

She grasped Ware's ass harder, trying to take more of him into her mouth, but he was like a mountain—unmovable. Her need to fill her mouth with him grew as her empty pussy contracted. Lifting her head, she pulled Ware deeper until he touched her throat, his long, hard texture building her tension. He gently pushed her head back to the pillow. God, the man must have control over every muscle in his body.

Nase groaned loudly. "That's it. I can't take any more. Erin, bend your knees."

She tingled with pleasure at his words. At least one of them was as ready as she was. Immediately, she did as she was bid and spread her legs apart farther. She expected Ware to move, but he remained where he was, the head of his cock in her mouth, his giant thighs keeping her pinned. She scored her teeth around his rim, more determined than before to make him come.

The feel of Nase's thighs beneath her own as he knelt surprised her, but the minute his cock head butted against her opening, she relaxed. She would have two cocks at once, more than she'd ever dreamed of.

She sucked hard on Ware, watching his face for a reaction. He gave no indication, but his stomach muscles rippled. She grinned around him, her teeth holding him in place. Then Nase's large hands gripped Ware's shoulders from behind, and she held her breath.

Nase didn't plunge in as she expected, as she wanted. Instead, he slowly entered her, his hard cock sliding in inch by inch, pushing her pussy wide, until his balls touched her. She couldn't move from her waist down, filled as she was by his cock and trapped by Ware's weight.

Ware tilted his hips and slowly pushed himself farther into her mouth.

Finally. She opened wider, tilting her head to take as much of him as she could. He hit the back of her throat and stopped. She closed her lips.

Neither man moved, keeping her pinned in two places. The helpless, excited feelings coursed through her as pleasure raced over every nerve. She tried to stay as still as they, but her pussy contracted at the eroticism of being filled to the maximum in both her mouth and core. Her heart raced and without meaning to, she found herself sucking on Ware.

He cupped her cheek as if to stop her, but instead he rubbed his thumb over her bottom lip. She couldn't believe Nase hadn't moved yet. She was on the edge of a massive orgasm and these two men were holding her there. The shards of excitement shooting from her core buzzed throughout her body, causing her to suck harder, breathe faster. She was so close and yet they waited.

Nase's strained voice broke the sound of her pants. "Ware."

It was the first time she'd heard him use that tone of voice, the same one Ware used with Nase. The command.

Ware dropped his head and took a breath as a tremor moved through his massive body. "Yes."

The simple word turned her world upside down. Nase and Ware both pulled out and moved back in. The rhythm was exact.

Both cocks retreating at the same time then pushing into her mouth and pussy, filling her only to leave again. The pace increased, pushing harder, sending shock waves of pleasure through her, flowing over her, around her and throwing her into her orgasm.

She closed her eyes as her scream vibrated Ware's cock even as her pussy tightened. A thousand lights exploded in her head as her body shook in ecstasy. Nase's shout came at the same time.

Ware pulled out of her mouth, allowing her deep breaths but denying her the pleasure of his taste. He moved off her, switching positions with Nase, and before she understood what was happening, he pushed his cock against her opening.

Her slowing heart picked up speed. To finally have Ware inside her, filling her.

"Hey, Fiya. You're going to love this." Nase had taken a position next to her head and leaned his half-hard cock toward her mouth. Without hesitation, she pulled it to her and sucked him in to the hilt before he was completely stiff.

Ware's cock penetrated her pussy, sliding deeper and deeper until he hit her cervix. She gasped, but had little time to examine her sensitized sex before Nase's cock took all her attention. She tongued it to hardness, causing her to lose some of it as it grew.

Ware began to stroke in and out as Nase did the same. But with her hands free, she captured Nase's balls and held them, unable to believe how hard he was already. Ware's thrusts were steady, not increasing in speed, and she found her need building slowly. He held back.

Nase moved his hands to her nipples and squeezed. Pleasure raced from her hard tips to her pussy and she tightened around Ware. It was too much. His huge cock pushing into her tight sheath,

Nase's fingers on her nipples and his cock in her mouth, pumping against her tongue sent her back up on the ledge of orgasm. She closed her eyes, allowing her body to spiral higher. Then Ware stroked her clit with his finger.

She couldn't hold back, her body vibrated with so much stimulation. Her hips lifted against the pressure on her tight nub and the penetration of Ware and she let go again.

The low growl that issued from Ware sparked her skin and traveled into her pussy, pushing her orgasm harder, expanding it through every nerve ending. Vaguely she sensed Nase's balls tightening in her palm and his cock pulsing against her tongue. It wasn't until she swallowed his cum that it registered they had all reached their pinnacle at the same time, a second time for her and Nase.

Both men took their time exiting her body, but after they did, she still couldn't move. "Oh my God." Her words were only possible on an exhale, her lungs too greedy for oxygen to waste time on words. Her body was replete with satisfaction and her mind couldn't grasp a complete thought. Her heart slowed, but deep inside it attached itself to the men who had given her such pleasure. Was it normal to feel connected after incredible sex? How would she know? Her first sex partner had been less than experienced. Hell, back then she didn't even know what her clit was. She grinned.

Nase collapsed beside her. "Shit, that was heart-stopping."

She giggled. He'd taken the words right out of her mouth.

Ware lay down on her other side.

She opened her eyes to find him looking at her with concern. "Are you okay?"

She clasped his hand in hers, gathering strength from him to answer. "I'm more than okay."

He looked unconvinced.

Nase grasped her other hand and she moved her gaze to his. "Are you sure you're all right?" He was far too serious.

She opened her mouth to make a joke, but found herself compelled to be honest with him. "Yes. I'm just wiped out."

"I understand." He smiled smugly.

If she had the strength she'd swat him, but she was just too tired.

Ware pulled her up against his side, burying his arm under her to prop her head on his shoulder. She needed no prompting to cuddle alongside him.

Nase plastered his hard body against her back and butt, holding on to her across her waist.

Whatever she'd been thinking to go on a nude cruise, it wasn't this, but she was so glad she did.

CHAPTER EIGHT

Nase grinned as he swallowed his instant oatmeal with apples and cinnamon in it. He loved the sweet food they could eat while on Earth. Sugar was rare on Eden.

"You may not want to be grinning so broadly when she comes out of the bathroom. We will have to answer some hard questions."

Ware's stern look wouldn't lower Nase's spirits today. Why couldn't the man just enjoy his sugar-coated cereal for a moment? Yes, they would have to convince Erin that last night was right and that they were from another planet and that she had to come home with them to complete the bond…all right, so maybe they still had a few hurdles to jump over, but now that they were connected, or soon would be, it would all happen as he'd hoped. "I know. But the fact we have bonded to her takes some of the stress away. I'm confident—"

"Dammit!" The feminine voice from their bathroom didn't sound too happy.

Nase tensed as the pocket door was thrown open and slammed to its end. So maybe those hurdles were higher than he'd anticipated.

Erin stood in all her naked glory with her hands on her hips, looking at them as if they'd just committed a crime. "We didn't use protection last night. How could you not use a condom?"

Nase shrugged. "We don't have to use it. We have no diseases."

"And you know this how?" She glared at him.

He glanced at Ware. A little help would be appreciated.

His friend caught the hint. "Where we come from, no one has these diseases you speak of and we know you don't have them."

She stomped toward them and pulled out a chair at the four-person table, before flopping into it. "And how do you know that?"

Nase jumped in. "You haven't had sex with anyone but us." Ware shook his head and looked down at his empty cereal bowl.

"What?" Erin grabbed his arm, her nails biting into it uncomfortably. "And how would you know who I have slept with and who I haven't? In case you hadn't noticed, the first night we had sex, I wasn't a virgin."

Her statement penetrated his contented haze. "When did you lose your purity?"

She sat back, releasing his arm to cross hers over her breasts, hiding her rosy nipples from his view. "When I was sixteen, if you must know. It was on the beach."

Nase's stomach tightened. They thought they'd saved her for them and all this time she'd already been with someone. He looked to Ware for confirmation and at his nod, Nase jumped to his feet. He paced, uncomfortable with learning the woman he had loved for so long had sex with someone before him. How did Ware handle it?

"Nase?" Her confused tone only made him more crazed. She was theirs.

Ware helped him out. "Nase has very strong feelings for you. It is hard for him to know you've been intimate with someone else."

"And what about you?"

Nase paused to listen to Ware's response.

"I feel as strongly as he. I just show it differently."

Nase couldn't resist. "Or not show it." Ware's slight shrug had him pacing again.

Erin sat up straight. "So you said you couldn't have a disease because no one does where you come from. Where exactly are you from?"

Nase looked to Ware, who answered, "Eden."

"What country is that in?"

Nase moved over to her and knelt at her feet. "It isn't in a country. It's a planet. We live near Naralina on the planet Eden."

Her gaze turned eager before she shook her head, clearly hurt. "Don't play with me. I asked you a simple question. If you don't want to tell me, you don't have to make fun of me."

Nase shook his head, but it was Ware who laid his hand on her arm. "We would never do that to you. Nase speaks the truth."

Again, she looked hopeful before she stood, breaking away from their touch. "Stop it. This isn't fair. Just because I'm the geek who oversees the tech department for a science fiction television company doesn't mean you can play with me."

She stood with her back to them, disconnected. Ware rose and they each touched a shoulder. She glanced at them in turn, her crushed look spearing Nase to the core.

"Ware, we must show her."

"I don't know."

Nase turned her face toward him. "Fiya, we would never lie to you. Keep information from you for your safety, yes, but never would we lie to you. We will show you."

He looked at Ware and his friend nodded. Stepping away from her, they stood in the middle of the living room, a little more than three feet apart. Nase crossed his right arm over his chest and pressed his finger against his left rib. Ware did the same, only using his left hand under his right arm. The air between them shimmered and they stepped away, allowing her to look at the doorway to their home.

Nase pointed. "This is Eden, our planet. This portal is only possible when two worthy citizens are given the implants to open it."

Erin stared, her heart beating faster than when they'd had sex. It couldn't be. It was impossible. She stepped toward what could only be called a doorway. "How does it work?"

"It opens and we can step through." Nase paused, studying her. "Or it can be used simply to view an area, like right now. We have opened it above the ground so if anyone is in the area they will not accidently walk in. Go ahead, look."

What they were saying was impossible, and yet, her secret hope, her wildest dream, shimmered before her. Tentatively, she stepped closer. The land was a vibrant green, slightly humid, much like it was in the seas they cruised upon. The sun shone and she could hear animals in the plant life. "It's beautiful."

Ware let out a breath and she moved her gaze to him. "You love your home."

"I do."

She looked at Nase. "So do you."

He nodded. Her home was a townhouse at the end of a row. It had a small manicured patch of lawn that was tended by the groundskeeper. Their planet, if it wasn't a trick, was incredibly natural, real.

Nase grasped her hands and turned her toward him. "We know we have no diseases because there are none on our planet."

"None?"

From behind, Ware placed his hands on her shoulders. "None."

His touch and his tone relaxed her. "Okay. I guess I have to believe you." She tried to smile, but it was a bit shaky. She still couldn't believe what she'd always hoped, that other planets had life, that there were other civilizations besides man, that creatures lived full lives, could possibly be true.

The two men moved away and closed the portal. The living room of the suite was as it had been.

Her mind spun with questions. She wanted to know everything. She needed to—"Shit." She sat on the floor, her strength suddenly gone.

"Erin!" Nase kneeled next to her. "What's wrong?"

She shook her head. "I might be pregnant by two aliens."

Ware crouched down, his green eyes alight with an inner excitement. "Is it the right time?"

She looked at him blankly before her mind registered her last monthly. Counting the days, she shook her head. "No. At least I don't think so. I've never really needed to pay attention before."

Ware dropped his gaze and she had the strange feeling he was disappointed. That couldn't be. She certainly wasn't. She would worry about it until her next cycle started. Having a baby by these two men would be crazy. She didn't really know them and they were from another planet. Seriously, another planet.

She grabbed Ware's arm. "That thing you do when you cause pressure against my skin. That isn't a trick, is it?"

"No. I air-touch you. I have the ability to move air by looking."

"Oh, wow. That's what happened to Leo."

Ware's brows lowered. "I should have pushed harder." He looked like a disappointed child.

She grinned before she turned serious again and stared at Nase. "Can you do this air-touch too?"

He shook his head. "That's Ware's specialty. He is Wareson from the Kindred of Air. I am Nassic from the Kindred of Mind." He pointed to the spiral on his arm.

She stared at the mark. It was natural, not a tattoo. That made her almost afraid to ask. "Does that mean you can do something to people's minds?"

Nase turned away and mumbled, "A little." Was he embarrassed?

Ware clarified. "Nase can make others tell the truth."

She stared at him unbelievingly for a moment then faced Nase. "Make me tell the truth."

He shook his head. "It is not necessary. You already do."

True, but how would he know? "Very flattering answer, but it doesn't prove anything. You may be a good judge— Wait. You both know more about me than simply from the couple days we've been together. How did you find out? Did you have Craig tell you all about me with this ability of yours?"

Again the two men looked at each other. Ware rose and offered his hand to help her up. She accepted, but refused to be distracted.

He didn't release her. "We have much to tell you."

* * * * *

Erin sat on the beach waiting for Ware and Nase to return with drinks. They had scouted out this secluded spot on the cruise line's private island for her because they wanted her naked. She wasn't sure if it was because they liked looking at her body or some other reason. They had also refused to answer any more of her questions until after she'd moved everything out of her cabin. She had just learned every man on Eden was taught how to pleasure a woman, when they decided they wanted to take advantage of the stop to come to the beach since the next day the ship was at sea. These men could be as frustrating as they were satisfying.

She coated the front of her body with lotion, scanning the area before slathering the lotion on her nipples. She couldn't simply cover them, she had to play with them, bringing them to hard points. She was being so naughty, she glanced around again. Still alone, she dipped her hand between her legs and spread the lotion over her mound and outside labia. Feeling rays on skin that had never seen the sun before was erotic and her pussy grew wet.

A strange pressure brushed against her nipples and she looked up to find Nase and Ware in sight but still far away. She waved. The pressure moved lower, over her tummy and then over her thigh. Disappointed, she looked at them approaching. Of course, Ware couldn't see her pussy. What if… Smirking, she knelt, facing them, and spread her legs. The pressure jumped to her mound and pushed through her curls and against her clit. Her blood rushed to the spot, leaving her a bit lightheaded. Nase grinned. She'd give him more to smile about. She lifted her breasts with her hands and brushed her nipples with her thumbs.

Nase's smile disappeared and the pressure against her clit increased, moving backward and forward. By the time the men were within speaking distance, she was close to an orgasm. The friction moved faster, causing her pussy to constrict with pleasure. She pinched her nipples, watching Nase stare at her with open desire as her hips rocked of their own accord. She would come for him, for his enjoyment. Thrusting her breasts forward, she twirled her nipples, sending shocks of excitement to converge in her core. Her sheath contracted and the pressure on her clit stroked faster. She couldn't hold on any longer. Arching backward, she let her shoulders rest on the ground as she came, her hips pulsing against the air, her legs wide open to Nase's sight.

She whimpered as her muscles relaxed. The unexpected orgasm drained her in the heat of the sun.

Nase dropped down next to her. "You are so beautiful in your ecstasy."

She opened her eyes to see him still staring at her pussy. Ware stood next to him, his gaze on her face. His lips twitched. He and she had put on a show for Nase. She understood and suddenly felt as if she were one of them, like the many gazes the two men shared that she didn't understand. For the first time she and Ware had a connection.

She lifted her hand to Nase's face. "That was for you."

He held her hand against his cheek before he moved it down to his chest. "You are our agapaytos."

She sat up and crossed her legs. "What does that mean?"

"It is the term we use for the most important woman in our lives. I think it would be like a wife in America, though the more direct translation is 'beloved.'"

A thrill of joy and fear combined within her heart. She didn't know what she felt for these two men until she learned more, such as, could they even be called "men."

Ware settled himself on the other side of her. His calming presence and the fact that once again they sandwiched her, caused her to relax. He handed her a bottled water. "I can see in your eyes you have many questions. Ask and we will answer."

"Are you human or something else?"

"We are descendants of humans who were brought to Eden over a thousand years ago, but living on our planet has caused us to evolve differently with…abilities, though we have many similar traits and knowledge."

She studied Ware, his long hair, his angular bone structure. He resembled Native Americans she had met except for his eyes, they were larger, and he had a chest full of hair that she liked cuddling against. Nase, on the other hand, had no hair on his chest and didn't appear to shave to make it that way. His features were very different from Ware's, almost Roman looking. "Why did you come on this nude cruise?"

Nase replied. "To meet you."

That had not been the answer she'd expected. "Why?"

The men exchanged that look again. She had a sense it was used when they had to tell her something they didn't want to. What had Nase said, they would never lie to her, but they might try to keep the truth from her?

Ware took her hand in his. A habit she noticed he had when he wanted to comfort while providing disturbing information. How fast she had learned to read them.

"We came to meet you because we have known about you for many years. We first chose you when you were but seventeen and we were nineteen. Though you were of age, we had to wait, due to our advanced years. In the City of Naralina, a woman of seventeen may 'marry' as you would say it, but only if her partners are also seventeen. Because Eden takes longer to orbit our sun, our years are longer and we had to wait for our ages to move closer."

Nase took over. "And then Ware had concerns about what was going on in the city and then we were—"

"We were worried about what you would think." Ware's gaze was intense.

Erin held up her free hand. "Wait. You said you met me when I was seventeen. I don't remember meeting you. I know I would remember you."

Ware stroked the back of her hand with his thumb. "You didn't meet us, exactly. We stepped through the portal and left you a present. You accepted it. Then we checked on you every so often to make sure you were doing well. You were our chosen one."

She had more than one concern with their answer. "What do you mean checked in on me?"

Nase grinned. "When men receive approval to choose a woman from Earth, they watch her for at least a year or longer to be sure she is worthy. We do this using the portal. We watched you run track and help your sister move into her apartment. We did happen to catch your graduation from college. We also saw days when you simply went to classes or work."

Erin tensed. She'd been stalked by people from another planet, only never approached. What an interesting science fiction television show that would make, except an audience would think it too farfetched. "So you watched me?" At the men's nods a thought occurred. "All the time? Like when I was in the shower or when I slept or…" She swallowed as panic rose at her weekly masturbation ritual.

Ware brought his arm around her shoulders, his touch calming. "No, we did not impose upon your privacy. That is against Dickinson Law."

"Is that what your laws are called in your city?"

Nase grinned. "No, actually those are the laws put in place for the entire planet. There aren't many, but spying on women of Earth during their private time is specifically not allowed."

She felt a certain amount of assurance over that detail. "I like this Dickinson guy already."

Ware's hand left her shoulder and moved behind her. "Dickinson is not a man."

"You have women rulers? Even better." Ware hesitated and stroked her back.

"Some cities do. But Dickinson wasn't a ruler, she was a poet."

Erin stilled, uneasiness creeping into her heart. "Her name wasn't Emily Dickinson, was it?"

Ware nodded.

"No way." She shook Ware off and stood, backing away from them. "Are you trying to tell me a nineteenth-century poet somehow visited your planet and they named laws after her?"

Nase rose. "Yes. If it hadn't been for her, we may have destroyed each other."

Erin shook her head, the idea that Emily Dickinson, the recluse of New England, the lady of the death poems, the author of the poem she stole, had visited another planet was too much for her to take in.

"What's wrong? I thought you liked the Emily Dickinson poem we left for you to find." Nase took a step toward her. "That was her first draft. I know it was messy, but your planet had the final version."

They had given her the poem? The first draft? She didn't have to feel guilty? A thrill of pleasure at owning something so special suffused her body, causing her to flush.

Ware cocked his head and studied her. "I think it's time for a swim."

"A swim?"

Before she could switch gears, Ware had jumped up, scooped her into his powerful arms and strode into the turquoise waters.

"Ware, put me down. What is it you two have about picking me up to drop me in the water? I can wade in myself. I'm a big girl."

The corner of his mouth lifted just a bit. "I guess we're used to the rocks at the entries of our lakes at home. We forget the sand here is soft under your feet."

"Really?" As he gently released her into the water, her curiosity about their planet rose again. "And do you go swimming often?"

He looked away, but then she found herself splashed from behind. "Nase!"

"What? I'm just swimming." His look of innocence did nothing to exonerate him and she splashed him back. He sank beneath the clear water and swam toward her. She backed up but found herself against Ware's large body.

Nase surfaced in front of her and pressed her against Ware. "Hmm, I think I like this." His lips lowered to hers and she tasted salt water as his tongue dove into her mouth.

"I do too." Ware's voice brushed past her ear as his hands grabbed her hips and pulled her against his hard cock.

Her body responded quickly to so much male, her folds swelling. As Ware reached between her legs, Nase grabbed her hands in his. Ware's fingers moved quickly into her pussy, making her limbs feel as liquid as the water surrounding her.

Nase's cock pressed against her abdomen, letting her know both men were anxious to have her and God help her, she wanted them.

Ware's fingers moved to her clit and as if on cue, Nase's cock bumped against her opening. To have them this way, in the warm waters would be— "No." She spoke the word against Nase's tongue before she found the strength to twist her mouth away. "No. Stop."

Immediately both men froze. Ware's calming voice filled her ear. "What is it, Bedia?"

She swallowed hard against her racing heart. "We are not doing this again without protection."

Nase pulled away as if she had shot him. "Shit."

Ware removed his hand. "But we have proved to you we are not diseased."

She turned to face him, her pussy still wanting his touch. "I know, but I cannot become pregnant. I'm single. You two will portal back to your planet after this cruise, and I will be left with the consequences of our actions."

Ware stepped back. "I think I understand."

Her body still yearned for them, but her mind was in full control.

"Very well." Ware dove into the water and swam away, his powerful strokes taking him far from her too fast. The loss of his presence hurt. Somehow she had upset him. She looked around for Nase, but he too had put distance between them.

Her eyes watered. She missed their constant interest. How greedy she'd become. How dependent. Turning, she walked back to the beach. As she came out of the water, she noticed two other couples in their area, but her spirits were so low, she didn't think twice about having company. When she flopped onto her towel, her phone buzzed. She burrowed her hand into her bag and pulled it out. She had three text messages. It was her boss again. She couldn't deal with that. He'd never know if she was in cell phone range. There must be a tower on the island. Was there nowhere she could go on this cruise without cell service except the middle of the ocean?

She'd just thrown her phone in her bag when a shadow fell over her. She looked up, already knowing it wasn't Ware or Nase. "Craig."

"I can't believe you got nude. Guess I would have lost money on that bet."

Oh, the man just didn't know when to stop. She stood and squinted at him. "How dare you?"

"What?" He backed up a step. "I just saw you over here and wanted to ask you why you moved out of our cabin. That you were naked was a surprise, that's all."

She stepped toward him. "You set me up at the swingers' cocktail party. First you didn't tell me it was for swingers and second you told those men I liked to be forced. How dare you?"

Craig's look of surprise quickly turned to back pedaling. "Is that what they told you? That's not exactly what I said. I simply told them you played shy so they wouldn't wonder why you remained dressed."

She poked her finger against his tanned chest. "You used me. You have used me since before we came on this cruise. Yes, you 'needed me' for your own selfish reasons. 'Erin, please come on the cruise with me or they won't let me go.' 'Erin, I need you to come to the cocktail party with me.' But never once did you do anything for me. Friendships are about helping each other. It's a two-way street, buddy, and you have reached my dead end!"

Craig quickly stepped back in the sand and fell on his butt. Guilt was written all over his face, which gave her a measure of satisfaction.

He scrambled to his feet again and his face changed. "Friends? Really? Why do you think Kathy and Lisa won't talk to you? Because they *needed* you to make the arrangements for the Cancun trip. And speaking of needing you." He took a step closer. "How about Ernest? The only reason he gets promoted is because you do all his work for him. Sure, he makes you think he's doing you a big favor, but the fact is, you should have been promoted over him. Everyone knows it. But he tells you he *needs* you and you do his work. So don't go taking it out on me that you're a patsy."

She looked at him in stunned disbelief. He threw his hands up and walked off past the people watching. She could have brushed off his revelations, but when he said everyone knew she should have been promoted, something clicked. Was that what Ernest had done? Why he couldn't function without her for a week? She didn't want to accept it, but her gut told her it was true.

Her eyes itched as tears threatened. She was a patsy, a wet rug, a sucker. Why? Why did she take it? Why didn't she see it? She wasn't stupid. No, she was gullible, too willing to see the best in people.

Splashing behind her made her turn and Nase ran up from the water, his look thunderous. He grabbed her by the shoulders. "Are you okay? Did he hurt you? I'm going to kill that asshole."

"What? No. I'm fine."

Ware joined him, neither man breathing hard despite the distance they must have swam.

"I'm going to kill him anyway." Nase took a step past her, but Ware grabbed his arm and halted him. Nase growled. "He upset her. The man needs to be taken care of."

Ware's look was downright evil and Erin almost felt pity for Craig. Almost. Instead, her watery eyes dried and she looked askance at Ware. "What are you thinking?"

He lifted a brow. "How would you like it if not a single woman showed any interest in having sex with Craig for the rest of this cruise?"

"What do you mean? How can you do that? Will you spread a rumor he's gay? He can always say he's bisexual to counteract that."

Ware shook his head. "Just leave it to us."

She glanced at Nase. His shit-eating grin was all she needed. "I think that would be perfect."

CHAPTER NINE

Ware watched Erin check the knot on the belt of her robe for the third time. He placed his hand over hers. "If you make it any tighter you won't be able to get it off."

She slapped her hands down to her sides. "I know. I'm just a bit nervous about this."

He placed his hand on the small of her back as they followed Nase through the crowd of lounge chairs and naked bodies. He couldn't say he understood her shyness. Her body was perfectly shaped and even if it wasn't, it wouldn't matter. It was about being comfortable, at least for him. The required dressing for dinner and while in port made his skin feel smothered. Being nude as they were now was much better.

Nase stopped. "I think this will do."

Ware looked around. They were on the second-level deck near the front. It was breezier here but there were fewer lounges, only forty or so. "We'll get settled in if you want to grab some beverages."

"Don't have to ask me twice." Nase wiggled his brows before giving Erin a quick kiss on the lips.

"There are others already here." Erin looked worriedly around them and tucked her hair behind her ears. A couple lay at the very apex of the deck and another couple read on the starboard side.

"Yes, and I expect there will be more. Since we are out at sea today, every chair is bound to be filled. I can't imagine anyone wanting to stay inside, unless of course they are having sex."

Erin had been contemplating the couple reading when her head snapped up at his comment. "Do you think a lot of people will do that?"

He shook his head. "Not this early, but later I imagine they will, and if you are good at this, maybe we will."

Her eyes widened and she swallowed hard. "I'd like that."

Another couple came up the stairs. It was two women who held hands as they decided where to sit. He gestured toward them. "Then you better choose your place before these fill up."

"Okay."

He followed Erin as she headed for the port side near the back. Of course, as far away from the people already seated. He grinned slightly. "Why don't you lie on your stomach and I will put lotion on your back? Your skin there is very pale compared to the rest of your body."

She nodded stiffly.

"You will need to take the robe off for me to put this on you."

"I know." She fiddled with the knot, loosening it, but not undoing it.

He placed his hand on her face. "Erin. You are a beautiful woman, but your back really needs a tan."

"It does, does it?" Her pique was exactly what he'd hoped for. "Then you better not let me burn. I expect every inch to be covered."

He winked. "I promise, every inch."

Her face flushed before she finally untied the knot and quickly lay down on her towel.

Ware sucked in his breath. Her body called to him, making him hard. Her perfectly rounded ass led to her muscular runner's legs. He wasn't sure which he wanted more, her legs wrapping around him in ecstasy or her ass in his hands as he pumped into her. Where the hell was Nase with the beer?

After squeezing out a handful of lotion, he rubbed it between his hands and slowly spread it on Erin's back. Her skin was soft, reminding him of how it felt sliding into her tight sheath last night. He silently wished he could spread the lotion with his air abilities, but that wasn't possible. He carefully covered her arms down to her fingertips. His heart squeezed as she grasped his hand. Peeling her fingers from his, he added more lotion and circled her ass cheeks with it.

Tension filled him and his balls tightened as he spread her cheeks and added protection within her crease, just in case. As his fingers moved to the inside of her thighs, he gritted his teeth. The urge to cover her with his body and thrust his cock inside her was too strong.

"You look as if you could use this."

Ware started at Nase's voice. Lifting his gaze from the shadow between Erin's thighs, he stared at the beer.

"You better take it, Ware."

Blinking, he refocused his attention and grabbed the cold bottle. Tilting it, he gulped half before putting it down. Nase's knowing smile didn't help his mood. He lifted the lotion with his other hand and threw it at Nase as he stood. "You can do her legs."

"I'd rather do her pussy."

"I'm right here, gentlemen."

Nase sat next to her. "Believe me, we know."

Erin's grin warmed Ware's heart. At least they were now sure she could handle them. Eden's men were large in body size and sexual appetite. It probably came from having so few women on the planet. That Erin could enjoy them both was reassuring.

Ware sat on his own lounge chair and lathered up as he watched Nase rub suntan lotion on Erin's calves. His friend's relaxed manner had left the minute he focused on her, and it was satisfying to see his muscles tense under the strain of touching her. Ware downed the other half of his beer. At least he wasn't the only one sporting an upright cock now. Nase's equaled his own. To touch her and not complete the act was torture, the reason he swam so far the day before. Like Nase, he needed to work off the sexual build-up.

Erin lifted her head to look at Nase. "Tell me about your home."

Nase stilled at her request, his hands on her feet. He was in no condition to speak, so Ware answered. "It is a beautiful place, not unlike St. Martin in climate. There are many varieties of plants and the soil is rich for growing. We have a mineral that supplies all of our energy simply by its exposure to the sun, so we have no need of this protectant lotion because our atmosphere keeps the sun at bay. Our exchange is counted in rancels, which are backed by each city's largest export. Gold, silver, diamonds and crystals are so common as to be ignored. There are no diseases and Edenists live longer than Earth humans."

Her breathing slowed. "It sounds too good to be true. There must be some downsides."

He glanced at Nase, who had finished with Erin and chugged a beer himself. "There are. No place is perfect, but it's our home."

She mumbled something unintelligible before her breathing grew deep.

Ware pointed to the railing. Quietly, Nase rose and they moved beyond hearing distance of Erin.

"What is it?"

Ware studied his friend. "We only have a few more days left."

"No. We don't. We are bringing her home."

Ware shook his head. "Only if she agrees. Even if she does, we need to set her up to leave. She has strong ties here, her mother, her sister, her friends."

Nase gripped the rail. "I wouldn't worry too much about her 'friends'. If they are anything like Craig, she doesn't need them."

"Did you spread the word about Craig's problem?"

Nase grinned, loosening his hold. "Yes. Last time I saw the man, he was at the Lido Deck bar by himself. There wasn't another person within twenty feet of him. I guess having these STDs is pretty serious."

"Good." There was a certain amount of satisfaction in knowing Craig's purpose for coming on the cruise was thwarted. "She is going to need time to come to a decision. Taking her with us would be a huge change in life for her."

"I know."

Ware took a deep breath. "We should ask her tonight."

"Tonight?" Nase looked over at Erin and Ware followed his gaze.

In her sleep she had rolled onto her side, exposing her tanned skin directly to the sun and the sight was breathtaking.

Nase nodded. "Yes. I want to bring her home." He stepped toward her, but Ware grabbed his arm.

"Bringing her home will be dangerous until we get inside the compound walls. We need to open the portal almost a league away to avoid detection from the City of Naralina. We have no idea how many outcasts might be in the area."

Nase stared at him. "I would die for her if that is what it would take."

Ware closed his eyes a moment at what the loss of Nase would do to his soul. "No. If you die, there is no guarantee she'd be safe after you're gone. We must stay alive to protect her. Tonight when she's asleep, we open the portal and check on Haven."

"Agreed. Now we better get back to her before she burns under this sun."

"Go."

Ware remained where he was. His gut told him if Erin came home with them, they would be putting her life in danger. But their connection to her grew stronger by the day and he and Nase were caught. There could be no other woman for them now. The question was, which would be better for her, to remain on Earth, safe and without them or come with them where their lives in the jungle were under constant threat?

He watched as Nase woke Erin and handed her the tube of lotion. She immediately began smoothing it over her skin. He let out a relieved sigh. She chatted with Nase, completely oblivious to the fact that the deck had filled with people. If she could feel comfortable naked all the time, she would have a better chance of adjusting. No one wore clothes on Eden.

Nase pointed to him and she turned to look. He air-touched her cheek and she smiled, her eyes softening. The Crius help him, he was beyond love with this Earth woman. He'd truly found Nirvana.

* * * * *

Erin looked at her cell phone. Her sister had called six times in the last twenty-four hours, but didn't leave a message. That made her nervous. What if something was wrong with their mother? But wouldn't Trish leave a message? Not that Erin could retrieve her messages, because the ship was still out of cell service range.

Nase plopped down on the wide lounge next to her. Their private balcony had given them a beautiful view of the sunset. They'd celebrated her day out on deck with red wine, the breeze brushing her naked body lightly which had been soothing, until Nase had brought her phone because it flashed. Now she couldn't relax.

"What's wrong, Fiya?"

She put the phone down on the side table. "I don't know. My sister has called numerous times, but she didn't leave a message. I'm afraid something is wrong. I thought I liked being out of cell phone range, but now I'm just worried."

Ware leaned forward, his elbows on his knees. "Would you like to see your sister?"

"What?"

"Nase and I can open the portal to see if she is all right, but you mustn't step through no matter what you see."

Oh wow. She had expected to be worried for another eight hours. Now she had a chance to see if her sister and mom were okay and experience the portal again. "So you can open a portal to anywhere?"

Ware nodded. "It takes two Edenists with a chip to open a portal. But not every Edenist is granted a chip. You must be deserving of one. Nase and I can open a portal to many places as long as we have some knowledge of them. The more we know about a location, the better we can zero in on it."

"But how could you find her?"

Ware looked at Nase next to her. "Do you think we can find her sister?"

"I do."

Erin studied Nase. "You can find anyone?"

"No. But we can find those we are attached to. We are linked to you, so you just need to help."

Adrenaline shot through her and she jumped up. "Great! What do I do?"

Ware stood and escorted her toward the slider. "Come inside where we won't be distracted."

She readily let him lead her to the living area. Nase followed behind.

Ware sat her in the recliner and held her hand. Nase stepped up and took her other one. Ware's voice calmed her. "You need to think of your sister. What she looks like, how she acts, the sound of her voice, where she lives."

Erin did. She thought of Trish's whining voice and her constant chaotic life. Trish always needed something, generally money.

Nase pulled his hand away. "I can sense her."

They both stepped back and opened the portal.

Ware returned to stand next to her, laying a hand on her shoulder. "Remember, no matter what, you cannot step through."

She nodded, the lump in her throat too large for her to speak. A large building came into focus and at first she tensed. Was it a hospital?

The image cleared quickly and she recognized the row of condos. "That's where I live."

Nase smiled. "I always thought it a nice place."

The portal floated them through the walls until they looked down into her living room. "But why are we at my condo? That's not where my sister lives."

Trish came into view, two beers in her hand. "Here."

A man on the couch took one. "Thanks."

Erin gripped Ware's hand.

Trish sat next to the man and took a piece of pizza from the box on Erin's coffee table.

"It's real nice of your sister to let you stay here while she's away."

"Are you kidding? She needs me to stay. Very particular about her place not being left empty. What can I say, she's a little strange."

Erin sucked in her breath and let it out in a whisper. "She's not supposed to be there."

The guy shrugged. "Yeah, most people are."

"No, I mean she's a real geek." Trish shook her head. "She works for a science fiction television station. She loves all that space stuff. Personally, I'm more interested in ghosts."

"Yeah, like Casper."

Trish frowned. "No, like scary ones. Oh, never mind."

They sat quiet for a moment, eating.

Erin dug her nails into her palms.

The man turned to Trish. "So your sister works for a television station. That must mean she makes a lot of money."

Trish shrugged. "I don't know. Whenever I ask her for some, she gives it to me. She's a real softy for a sob story. That's where the pizza came from."

"She has good taste."

Trish shouldered him. "Hey, I picked out the pizza. She just paid for it. This was supposedly a new tire. I just have to tell her how much I need from her and she caves."

The man stilled and looked shrewdly at Trish. "So if I tell you I need you, will you cave?"

"That depends. What did you need from me?"

"I want your hot pussy for this hard-on I'm getting just thinking about it."

Trish giggled. "I thought you were hungry."

"I was, but I can finish after we fuck." He pulled her close.

Trish dropped her plate on the coffee table.

"I've seen enough." Erin's chest hurt and she wanted to cry, but her anger at her sister wouldn't let her.

Ware and Nase quickly closed the portal. Ware pulled her up out of the chair and held her. "I'm sorry you saw that."

She lifted her face from his chest. "I'm not. I never thought my own family member would be so dishonest. If I can't trust my family or my friends, who can I trust?"

Nase stepped behind her and pressed his body gently against hers. "You can trust us. We would never betray you. You mean too much to our hearts."

She looked up at him. "I do?"

He nodded. She looked at Ware and he nodded as well.

"Wow." The warmth in her heart was a new feeling and she wasn't quite sure what it meant, but the fact these two gorgeous men felt something for her had to be a good thing.

Nase kissed her cheek. "In fact, we have something very important to ask you."

"Okay."

Ware kissed her other cheek. "We would like you to consider coming back to Eden with us."

"What?" Her heart shifted into overdrive. "Go to your planet?"

Nase squeezed her waist. "Yes. We want to spend a lot more time with you."

Her mind raced. What would it be like? How did they live? Would she have to keep it a secret? What would she do there? Could she come home? How long would she be away? What about her job?

Ware stared at her and air-touched her hair away from her face like a gentle breeze. She took a deep breath. "I would love to go home with you, but I have so many questions."

Nase yelled, grasped her against him and kissed the back of her head. "You made my day, Fiya."

Ware touched her shoulder. "It's not a vacation we speak of. We feel so strongly for you, we want you to come live with us. However, you can come back and visit your family and friends when you wish to."

Live with them? Erin pulled away from both men and sat on the couch. "Oh wow." She couldn't believe this. Everything she dreamed of was just dropped in her lap. She glanced at the two men who watched her cautiously before she returned her gaze to her hands. Actually, she'd only hoped for one man. Had never known two was a possibility. Who was she kidding? She didn't know living on another planet was a possibility, despite wanting it with all her being.

She looked at them again, her personal dream come true. Then reality set in. She had a job, a condo, her mom, her sis— Anger returned. Her sister had used her. Had everyone?

Ware knelt down in front of her and took her hand, his touch loosening her tension, allowing her to think. "Erin, you do not need to answer now. This is a life-changing request we ask of you and it needs more than a few minutes contemplation. You will have questions and concerns and we want to tell you everything you want to know. But for tonight, simply know we are yours for as long as you will have us."

Nase dropped down on the couch next to her. The man never simply sat. Everything was done to the fullest extent. He gave her shoulders a squeeze. "We, of course, hope you will want us forever, but we'll take what we can get." He winked, but she sensed the sincerity of his words.

"I promise you I will think about it. In fact, I doubt I'll be able to think of anything else."

Nase frowned and removed his arm. "That's not good. I had hoped to help you forget your troubles with some hot sex. What do you think, Ware?"

Ware's small, sensuous smile had her body tightening again in anticipation of his touch. "I think that's an excellent plan."

CHAPTER TEN

Erin noticed Ware no longer grasped her hand, but rather her leg. Her heart beat faster at the hope he would move it toward her pussy. He didn't disappoint, smoothing his way up her inner thigh until he touched her outer lips, but then he stopped.

She snapped her gaze to his and swallowed at his sharp-eyed look. "I think I will watch for a while." He removed his hand and lounged back on the floor.

No air brushed her body. How could he make her wet and then step away? She could never do that.

She looked to Nase, who shrugged. "Guess we'll have to give him a show then, won't we?"

Fire flew through her veins at the idea. She nodded, anxious to start but no clue as to what she should do.

"Get on your hands and knees."

Not exactly what she had expected, but her pussy already ached to be touched so she was agreeable. She knelt and then assumed the position Nase requested, but he angled her so Ware could see them from the side. Then he moved to her other side and crawled under her.

"What are you doing?"

"I'm enjoying the view." He stared at her breasts.

If he wanted to tease, then she could too. "You know they taste as good as they look."

"Ah, Fiya, you don't play fair."

She wanted to tell him she didn't play at all, but then his mouth latched on to her nipple. The sensation was exquisite as he sucked lightly before nibbling at her hardened peak.

She glanced down at his stomach where his muscles had tightened when he lifted his head and moaned.

He let his head fall back. "Ware, do you think these are hard enough yet?"

She looked at the massive man watching them.

"No, not yet."

Her stomach tensed in anticipation just before Nase used his fingers to grasp her nipples and gently tweak them. "How about now?"

Ware shook his head.

Nase sighed. "He can be so hard to please."

Moisture pooled between her nether lips, her body signaling her need to be filled. When Nase pulled and pinched at her nipples she threw her head back. Spirals of pleasure wound down to her core, causing her legs to widen. "Yes."

"Now." Ware's voice shot through her excitement and she took a few deep breaths while Nase pulled himself out from beneath her and grasped her hips. "Hey, Ware, throw me the Shilla.

She looked back to see Nase catch a small bottle of liquid. "What's that for?"

"You'll see."

"And you'll use protection." She didn't make it a request.

"Argh. If you insist."

She grinned. "I do."

As a condom flew through the air, she let her head drop between her arms. Out of the corner of her eye she caught the empty condom wrapper dropping onto the rug. Nase's aversion to condoms, but willingness to wear them for her, was endearing. Maybe she could go on the Pill when she returned home. She much preferred feeling him inside her without the thin barrier. Just the idea had her blood racing again until warm liquid slid down her butt crease. "What are you doing?"

"Relax." Nase's hand on her ass was like a person settling an animal. "I'm just enjoying the view right now. Seeing what you like."

The liquid had a slight tingling sensation. Nase's finger traced her crease right to her ass opening. She pulled forward.

"Whoa, where are you going?"

She looked back at him. "You're in the wrong place."

His grin was downright diabolical. "No, I'm not. I'm exactly where I want to be."

Oh God. He wanted to touch her *there*.

"You'll only know what you like if you try it. I want to please you in so many ways. Will you let me?"

She looked at Ware, whose gaze was intense. His whole body stiff with anticipation, especially his cock. That she could turn on these men so much still surprised her. She dropped her head again. "Okay."

Nase gripped both her ass cheeks in his large hands and massaged. Her muscles relaxed under his ministration. Then one finger moved down her crease again, spreading the warming liquid until it covered her anal opening.

Nase continued to massage her ass with his other hand. "Stay loose." Hearing his voice soften with expectation had her body listening.

As his finger penetrated her opening, a wild zing of excitement shot from there to her clit. She tensed at the enticing feeling and Nase's hand moved in circles again, though the finger remained still. She took deeper breaths to help her enjoy the new experience.

The finger, barely inside her, moved deeper and again her clit reacted and her pussy tightened.

She turned her head to look at Ware as he always helped calm her, but he looked like a statue, his muscles hard with tension.

"Play with her pussy, Nase. She needs something else."

Erin expected Nase to remove his hand from her ass, but instead, he simply touched his cock to the opening of her sheath. A thrill shot up her spine as he slowly moved it inside, just a bit.

Her heart pounded, her body anxious for full penetration.

"Now let me in, Fiya." As Nase spoke, he pushed his finger deeper into her ass. The stimulation traveled straight to her clit and her pussy tightened around him in pleasure.

"Ah, that's it." He moved his cock farther inside and then inched his finger in more.

She was panting now with her need. "Nase. Do it."

At her words he thrust his cock all the way inside to her cervix as his finger pushed all the way inside her ass.

She lifted her head, the dual sensations spiraling out of control throughout her body. "More," she gasped.

Nase didn't hesitate. Leaving his finger buried, he began to pump into her. Every thrust sent multiple shocks circling her pussy and her anal entrance. Each spasm wound her tighter until she screamed as her body convulsed around him.

His yell followed, his hand gripping her hip. When he slowed, he eased his finger out and patted her ass. "Did you like it?"

She dropped her head and shrugged. "I'm not sure. I might have to try it again."

Ware hissed and she looked at him. His eyes were closed, his hands in fists, his cock hard.

Nase chuckled. "Be careful what you wish for."

Ware was on her before she could catch her breath, pushing her down onto the rug, his cock pressing between her thighs. To have Ware lose control sent excitement ricocheting through her. She wanted him to take her now.

He rocked his pelvis against her ass as if on instinct alone, his cock brushing her thighs, teasing but not fulfilling. His low growl brushed past her ears, his hips lifting as he probed her entrance. The hardened muscles of his chest rubbed against her back.

She held her breath as Ware's cock found her opening.

He plunged in hard, to the hilt.

The pleasure shattered her and she screamed as another orgasm hit her unexpectedly.

Ware stilled. "By the Crius, woman. You push my limits."

She vaguely registered his words, too satiated to focus on them.

When he pulled out as quickly as he'd entered and lay down next to her on his back, she couldn't help the disappointed sigh she released. She opened her eyes finally to enjoy the view.

Ware's eyes were closed, but his stomach was rippled with tension and his cock stood straight and hard. He hadn't come!

He was trying to calm himself. She didn't want him calm, she wanted him frenzied like she and Nase.

She lifted up and crawled between Ware's legs, careful not to touch him. She leveraged herself to straddle him.

His eyes opened and she speared herself on his upright cock. His fullness spread her slick inside and electric shocks spiraled from her center, spreading across her abdomen.

"Ah Bedia. That is too good."

She nodded, unable to speak yet, but she was in total agreement. The sensations were amazing.

Ware held her hips, keeping her still.

Nase strolled across the room and sat on a recliner to watch. His hot gaze roamed her body, causing her to squeeze her sheath involuntarily.

Ware's fingers dug into her. "No." The word was pushed through gritted teeth.

She dropped her gaze to meet his, but the intense desire in his eyes had her tightening again.

"Please, I won't be able to hold back and I want to pleasure you."

She cupped his cheek. "You already do. Let me do this."

He looked so uncertain. What had his life been like for him to be so unwilling to give up control? She easily imagined a young Ware, completely calm and sitting politely while others boys ran around a room, yelling and playing.

"Please, Ware."

He gave the barest of nods. She moved her hand from his cheek and rubbed it across his large pectoral muscles, stroking his tight nipples. He obviously held on, although he'd let her take over.

She looked at Nase again. "Throw me a condom please."

The man rolled his eyes, but did as asked. She had to bite her lip to keep from laughing at him. As she caught the condom, she moved and Ware groaned. He really was on the verge. Quickly, she lifted herself from him and he released his breath in a hiss. Sheathing him with the rubber, she slowly lowered herself again, this time enjoying every inch as the pleasure of him washed over her.

Once seated, she checked his face. His jaw was tight, his eyes closed. She no longer needed to come with him. She just wanted to bring him to his climax. Lifting his hands, she placed them on her breasts. He gently massaged them, but didn't open his eyes.

Erin leaned her chest toward him as she bowed her back, moving her hips forward and letting her head fall back.

Ware's hands tightened on her, each hand encapsulating a breast. His exhaled breath was loud, but he didn't break. Slowly, she moved her hips back and then forward again, keeping the two of them pelvis-to-pelvis.

His hands stopped kneading.

She grinned. She wanted this for him, but it felt so good, she wasn't sure she could hold on to her control. Again she moved her hips backward and forward, rubbing her clit against him as his cock swelled within her.

She kept the pace steady, watching Ware's reactions, holding back her own. As she edged closer to fulfillment, she wanted more, so she reached behind her and cupped Ware's balls.

His groan was her only warning. His hands left her breasts and grabbed her ass, holding her tight against him as his hips bucked upward, pushing so deep she exploded. The air around her glowed with colors as pleasure swept her up to dizzying heights. Slowly, the falling pieces of her orgasm settled, and she fell forward onto Ware's chest.

Eventually, he lowered his hips, and she slipped to his side. He grasped her to him, and love seeped into her heart. This is where she wanted to be. These men were her destiny. They had broken her years of uncertainty and proved to her she was desirable. They treated her better than she deserved, better than her friends' boyfriends treated them. Ware and Nase were truly, literally out of this world.

She grinned against Ware's chest. More out of this world than she ever expected.

He tipped her chin up. "You broke me." His face was far too serious.

"No, I freed you."

He studied her, concern plain in his eyes. "Freed? No, I fear now I am truly enslaved."

She didn't like that at all. "Well, if you are, then I guess I am too."

"And me." Nase sat on the floor next to them.

"Good. We can all be addicted to one another." She held her hand out to him and he promptly put it on his already hardening cock. She laughed, filled with a happiness she'd never experienced before.

"If you are bound to us," Nase wiggled his brows, "then when you come to Eden, we won't have to block your pheromones because all men will sense you are taken."

Erin stiffened. "What do you mean, block my pheromones?"

Nase winked. "On Eden we have far more men than women. Actually, it is a Dickinson Law that every woman must bond with at least two men."

"Seriously? You let a reclusive woman poet instigate that law?" Respect for her favorite author grew.

Nase frowned. "It is an important law. But since we have very few females, many unclaimed women often have their pheromones blocked to avoid being overwhelmed with propositions."

"Nase, we should go to bed now." Ware's voice held a warning note she recognized, but she wouldn't let him stop Nase this time.

Erin sat up, a nagging suspicion demanding to be answered. "So these women asked to have their pheromones blocked so men won't be interested in them sexually?"

"Exactly. But since you're claimed, you won't need that."

Her body heated as anger spread through it. "But that's what you did when you first claimed me, when I was seventeen?"

"We couldn't bond with you yet, so I blocked your pheromones so you wouldn't be bothered by Earth humans. We didn't begin the bond with you until the other night."

Erin stood and stepped away from Ware, keeping her gaze on Nase. "So all those years I thought I wasn't attractive, wasn't sexy, were because of something you did to me without even asking me? All those years I had no one to have sex with. No one to hold me and make me feel cared for. All those years I was alone and lonely were because of *you*."

"I did it for you, for us. To keep our relationship pure."

Her eyes watered as the betrayal set in, but she didn't care. "So why now? Why did you wait? Why not come to me five years ago? Surely twenty-three is old enough on Eden to marry?"

Ware stood. "I wouldn't let him."

"What?" Her heart couldn't take more. The tears flowed freely down her face. "Why?"

"The timing wasn't right and then," he looked away, "then we were banished from Naralina and had to make our home in the jungle and it wasn't safe."

She shook her head. "But you still live in the jungle. Why now?"

"Because we need you, Fiya." Nase stood and stepped forward, his arms out. "We have built our own compound. We can keep you safe. We cannot go on without you any longer. And if we do not bring you back, our leadership will be questioned."

"Oh God." She shook as her fantasy story splintered around her. "You needed me? Like Craig needed me. Like my sister needed me. To use me. Who cares what I need?" She started to hiccup as her anger took over her hurt. "I'll tell you who cares—hic—I do. I don't need—hic—to be needed. I need—hic— to be *wanted*."

Ware took a step forward. "Bedia—"

"Don't." She stuck her hand out as if she had the power to stop such a powerful man. "Don't come near me. You—hic—gave me hope in so many ways—hic—only to destroy it, which—hic—is worse than having no hope at all. Hic—I can't even stand to — hic—look at you. I'm leaving."

She had no idea where she would go or what she would do, but she had to get out of the suite, away from them. Grabbing her robe from the back of the chair in the kitchen and her purse from the counter, she ran from the cabin. She didn't want to stop for an elevator so she took the stairs two at a time as far up as she could go until her breath gave out.

Opening the door of that deck, she stumbled out and collapsed on a lounge chair. Sobs racked her body, overwhelming the hiccups, the pain in her heart too much to bear. She wished for numbness, sleep, anything to relieve her agony.

"We need to go after her." Nase headed for the door.

"No."

"Yes. She needs us."

Ware stepped in front of him. Didn't he realize what they had done? "No. What she needs is to be away from us. Didn't you hear what she said?"

"Of course I heard, but she doesn't know what she needs."

"And you do?"

Nase stilled. "Shit, I don't have a clue."

"Exactly. We thought we were doing what was right for her, but we messed up her life."

Nase paced to the other end of the room. "No, you messed her up because you kept saying we needed to wait. We wouldn't have even come here if she hadn't taken this nude cruise. It was the only way I could convince you. We *should* have bonded with her five years ago."

"Waiting until it was safer wouldn't have been a problem if you hadn't blocked her pheromones."

"So I'm the one at fault here?" Nase turned away and strode out onto the balcony.

Ware understood exactly what he felt. Guilt, hurt, anger, frustration. They churned inside him too, whirling around like a tornado waiting to take out anything in its path, including Nase.

He gritted his teeth, trying for his blasted control, but all he could see in front of him was Erin's face. The shock and hurt of their revelations too much for her. Despair flooded his senses. To have waited so long, followed what he thought was the right course of action only to learn he'd made such a heart-wrenching mistake was too much.

Without thinking, he slammed his fist into the table.

The sound of breaking wood brought Nase in from outside. "What are you doing?"

Ware spun. "Losing control. That's what you wanted from me, isn't it? Does it make you happy?"

"No. It doesn't help us now. Now is when you need to think of a way to get her back."

"Then I guess you'll have to think of a way."

Nase stalked into the kitchen and grabbed him by the shoulders. "Ware. She's the most important part of our lives. You can't give up now."

Ware broke Nase's hold. "It's over. Don't you see? She doesn't want us."

"By the bowels of Bangley you don't mean that."

Ware stared at Nase and shook his head. "We don't deserve her."

CHAPTER ELEVEN

Nase backed away from the man he'd always thought of as a true brother. He wanted to hit him, knock him down, punch him until his sense returned. "You may be right, but the fact is we still want her. We need to fight for her."

"How are we supposed to do that? We can lay waste to every man on this ship, but it won't bring her back."

Nase gripped the back of the now table-less chair. "Not fight other men. We need to convince her of how much we love her. That we will care for her with every breath. That we will do whatever it takes to have her in our lives."

Ware fisted his hands. "And will that make up for eleven years of loneliness? I know what it feels like to be alone."

That Ware was an only child had haunted him until the day they had met. He, on the other hand, unfortunately had four brothers, all who couldn't have cared less about him after their mother died. Shit, they were so like his father, they didn't care about their own mother's death. She had been nothing more than a baby maker to them. But to Nase, she had been his world. "And you think I don't know what it is to be alone? Is that what you're saying? I can't possibly know what Erin is feeling?"

"Do you?" Ware took a step forward. "Do you know how many nights she felt unwanted, crying herself to sleep when a man she liked rejected her because of us? Because of us!" Ware punched his own chest.

The vision Ware painted of Erin tore through Nase's anger and he stepped back from the rage in Ware's eyes. He'd seen Ware angry at himself a number of times because the man held himself to impossible standards, but this was far worse. And for once, he understood. They had taken something precious from the most important person in their lives because they had been too focused on themselves.

Nase fought the urge to give in to Ware's despair as it crept around his heart. They had failed. In trying to do what was right for Erin, they had made her life miserable. They couldn't go back and change what they had done. Even the Crius didn't have that ability.

"See?" Ware's voice had turned smug, filled with self-loathing. "Even you admit to what we have done to her. There is no going back. I say again. We don't deserve her."

"But we can't live without her. She is our bonded agapayto."

Ware turned away and spoke over his shoulder. "But she can live without us here on Earth. We can give her that. Allow her to have a husband and children. If we truly love her, we will let her go."

"No!" Nase slammed the chair down, ignoring the shattered pieces as slivers of wood shot into his shins. He welcomed the pain, his mind feeding off the adrenaline of it. "No. We can't take back what we have done, but we can make up for it. The only way to do that is to convince her we will spend the rest of our lives doing so."

"Let her go, Nase."

He spun on his heel and headed for the door. "Not a chance. She always wanted one special man to make her happy. Well, we have something more. We have two."

He opened the door and looked back at Ware. The man stood like a bronze statue among the chaos of splintered wood, his eyes soulless.

"We will get her back. I promise you. I will never give up. And when you are ready to fight for her, I will welcome your help."

As he strode through the door, a new determination filled his heart. He would find a way to win Erin's heart again, for both of them.

* * * * *

Erin sipped her cup of tea. The lounge chair she'd slept on last night had become her new home. It wasn't as if she had any clothes or toiletries because they were still in Ware and Nase's suite. She had no idea how she would retrieve them. She'd have to eventually, but she couldn't think about that yet.

She was thankful the boat was docked in Jamaica because people went ashore, leaving the decks above the pool sparsely populated. She may fit in fine with her robe, but she doubted her tear-streaked face was a welcome sight.

Her stomach constricted around the warm liquid as she took another sip. Breakfast was not an option. She had a hangover but it wasn't from alcohol. She'd had too much of a good thing. She should have known there was no way Nase and Ware could be for her. Their bodies, personalities, even being from another planet, were all too perfect. She should have known there was a catch.

But she thought them different. She thought they *wanted* her. She was so stupid. What else had she been naïve about? Craig said her boss and her friends. Great. If that were true, she didn't have much to look forward to once she returned home.

She just had to survive two more days.

A buzzing in her purse caught her attention. She must have cell service again. Pulling out her phone, she answered, "Hello."

"Hey, sis, how's the cruise?"

A new tension ran through her and she set down the tea. "It's great. I'm getting lots of sun, dancing the night away, and relaxing."

Her sister hesitated. "Well, that's great. I wish I could be there. Instead I got a ticket for overnight parking in that lot where I had the flat tire. They told me they would tow the car if it wasn't gone in twenty-four hours, but they never said I'd get a ticket. It's for forty dollars. Can you believe it?"

Erin squinted as she kept her voice normal. "No, I can't believe it. I can't believe you got a flat tire and didn't have the money to pay for it. I can't believe you are staying in my condo and buying pizza and having sex on my couch."

"What? Oh my God, you've been spying on me!"

"Who me? But I'm just a softy. Why would I do that?"

"You *were* spying on me. How dare you?"

Erin couldn't control her voice any longer. "How dare I? How dare you? You tell me you need this and you need that and milk money from me every week. But you're just using me. That ends here and now. Get out of my condo and go figure out your own finances because this bank is closed!"

Trish stuttered on the other end of the phone, her own heavy breathing coming through loud and clear. "Fine. But if you're going to cut me off, you better cut off Mom too, Miss Perfect. Mom has six friends plus me who she complains to besides you, but she makes you think she 'needs' to tell you everything because she has no one else she can confide in. That's what you thought, wasn't it? That you're the special daughter? You are such a sap."

Erin gasped as the pain of her mother's betrayal sliced through her heart, but quickly hardened and turned cold. "You're right, I was a sap, but not anymore. I'm sending the police over to my condo tonight and if you are still there I will have you arrested for trespassing."

"You wouldn't."

"Oh, I will. And Trish, don't call me for bail either." Erin ended the call and dropped her phone on the lounge. It flashed, indicating there were messages, but she ignored it. Tears welled up and threatened to fall. How the hell could she produce more tears? She had to be dehydrated by now. She looked accusingly at the innocent cup of tea on the little table next to her. Was she really mad at a cup of tea? She shook her head. She was losing it.

There was only one common denominator with her relationship breakdowns and that was her. She *had* been a sap. She let people walk all over her, use her, play on her sympathies. Was it because she wanted to be liked? Was it because Nase had kept her from having a normal, healthy sexual relationship? Was it because she'd been denied that for too long by Ware?

She picked up the tea again and took a sip. If that were the case and her pheromones were back in place, maybe it was time to find her backbone. She picked her phone up and checked the messages. Fourteen texts from Ernest. She read the first text from four days ago. "Seriously?" How did the man turn the computer on in the morning if he couldn't fix a simple purchase link? Craig's words echoed in her mind. *The only reason he gets promoted is because you do all his work for him.*

She sneered. This would be a good test of Ernest's capabilities. She closed the message and threw her phone back into her purse. Screw it. She was done helping everyone else. It was time to help herself. She took another sip of tea, her stomach loosening a bit. Glancing around the deck, she noticed only a few people on the other side. Unbelting her robe, she let the morning sun warm her. She'd buy more lotion in one of the shops in a little while. She wasn't ready to face Nase and Ware yet. Her heart hurt and just thinking of them made her stomach rumble.

Finishing the tea in hopes it would help her stomach, she lay back and focused on the heat of the sun on her bare skin. Ware could cool her off with his air-touch, but more likely he'd heat her up at the same time.

She tried to focus on something else. Nase's recitation of Emily Dickinson as he held her in the water came to mind. God, there were other exciting spots in her life besides those two! There had been the adrenaline rush the day she found the original poem by Emily Dickinson, *Wild nights! Wild nights!* Exactly what she had with Ware and Nase.

A change in temperature on her skin had her opening her eyes. Nase stood in front of her as if she'd summoned him.

"Erin. I want to talk to you." No grin curved his lips, a strange occurrence for him, but she wasn't exactly happy either.

"I don't want to talk to you." She wrapped her robe about her again.

Nase wouldn't take the hint, but that didn't surprise her. He sat on a neighboring lounge chair and faced her. "I have to talk to you. You misunderstood. We have wanted you for so long, it has become a need of our hearts, our souls. I love you, Erin."

She shook her head. She didn't want to hear this.

"I think you might love me as well. Do you?"

A strange sensation pushed her mind as he forced her to tell the truth. "I don't know how I feel about you right now."

His face fell.

She ignored the tug at her heart. "Getting the truth doesn't always mean it will be something you want to hear."

"I know. But I told you we would only be honest with you and we have."

"You also told me you might not tell me everything. That means you could love me while on this cruise but not at home. How can I trust what you say?"

Nase leaned forward and she leaned away.

"Please, Erin. We chose you years ago. We want to bring you home to be our agapayto. We cannot live without you."

"But I've only known you for a few days. How do I know there isn't another man out there that would be my soul mate? I haven't had the chance to know the joy and heartbreak of any relationship, except this one. I don't even know if I would recognize love when I was in it because I've never felt strongly for a man. Hmm, I wonder why that is."

"I only blocked your pheromones because I couldn't stand to have another man touch you. You were destined for me and Ware."

Erin looked away from him. His intense gaze was too much. His honesty was too much. It hurt, while at the same time it made her furious. "Go away, Nase."

"Erin—"

"I believe the lady asked you to leave."

At the somewhat familiar voice, she turned back toward Nase to see Adam, from the swinger meet and greet, standing on the other side of the lounge chair.

Nase turned around. "We're talking."

"No, I think you're done. The lady asked you to go away."

Nase stared at her, his face hard, but she refused to encourage him. Standing, he fisted his hands. Would he take his anger out on Adam? The older man may be fit, but next to Nase, every man appeared small…except Ware. Nase finally turned and stalked away. She couldn't help watching him, torn by her feelings for him and the hurt he caused her.

She looked at Adam and attempted a smile, but it didn't quite work. "Thank you."

"Is this chair taken?"

She shook her head. "Where's Len?"

Adam laid out his towel and sat. "He's getting a spa treatment. I'm not sure if today is the massage or the facial."

"Maybe that's what I need."

"If you need to be pampered, I highly recommend it."

She played with the belt of her robe. The fact was, Ware and Nase treated her like a queen, but after their betrayal maybe she did need a little pampering. Maybe some new clothes too and then she could delay going to their suite for her belongings.

Adam's hand on her arm surprised her.

"Are you okay?"

"No. But I'm sure I will be eventually."

"I don't mean to pry, but I thought you and that gentleman were together. Did you have a fight? Did the other luscious hunk come between you?"

She stared, uncomprehending, for a moment. "Oh, no. No, those two are a package deal."

Adam sighed. "Nice package."

Her lips quirked up of their own accord. "Nice packages actually."

He grinned, but didn't ask any more questions and lay down on his lounge.

Yes, Nase and Ware would be any woman's wet dream, but a relationship was based on more than that, wasn't it? How would she know? Her stomach tightened again. "Adam, how long have you and Len been together?"

"Eighteen years now."

"Was he your first long-term relationship?"

He turned to face her. "He was for me. Len had been in three before us."

"How do you know it's the one?"

He shook his head. "You don't know it. You feel it. With Len I feel loved, respected, fulfilled. I make him feel the same way. We complete each other."

Erin frowned. "But didn't you feel this way with others you were with?"

Adam sat up and faced her. "No. I kept hoping the next man would be 'the one'. Even tried to force it a few times, but I was fooling myself. After a while, I gave up. There is nothing worse than wanting something so much and never getting it."

"Tell me about it." She rolled her eyes.

"Then you understand. I had decided to stick to emotionless one-night stands and then Len turned me down." He smirked. "I don't know if it was my male ego or his hot body, but I became determined to catch him."

"Why did he turn you down?"

Adam chuckled. "He says because I thought too much of myself, but the truth is, he'd just ended a long-term relationship and was afraid to try again. He said he spent too many years as a square peg in a round hole. Wouldn't it be nice if the first relationship we were ever in was the perfect one? Life would be so enjoyable then, and we wouldn't have so much baggage."

First relationship. That's what she had, but was it "the one"? "But if that were the case, wouldn't you always wonder if there was someone else out there better suited to you?"

Adam shook his head. "Not if it was the right person." His brow furrowed for a moment, making him look more his age. "Is that what you're trying to figure out with those hunks of yours, if it is the one?"

She looked away. Were they?

A shadow fell across her and it wasn't Nase. Her ability to sense that was a bit disturbing. Looking up, she found a man more her age than Adam's, with short dark hair and a tattoo on his right shoulder. Dog tags hung against his very tan chest.

"Excuse me, but I was wondering if you would like this BBC I bought. I saw you sitting here talking to Adam and it just seemed like the perfect drink for you."

Of all the pick-up lines, that had to be pretty original. She may not have heard many, but her male friends used a slew of them. "And what is a BBC?"

He crouched down and a whiff of musk caught her attention as did his "package." "It's banana, Bailey's and coconut."

Wow, that really did sound good. "But it's still early morning. A drink this early?"

"You're on vacation. Be rebellious."

The banana and coconut were fruits, after all. "Okay. Thank you."

He handed her the drink and gave her a winning smile. Truly the man was very attractive.

Adam cleared his throat. "Erin, this is Michael."

Michael moved to sit next to Adam. "Nice to meet you."

She took a sip of the drink and closed her eyes as the cold liquid moved down to hit her empty stomach. "Hmm, that is really good. She opened her eyes to find Michael staring at her and Adam grinning. "What?"

Adam answered her. "Nothing."

"So, Michael, are you a swinger too?"

The man snapped out of his stare. "What? No. No, I just know Adam from the show last night. We were in the same row."

"Oh." She took another sip and covertly eyed the man as he talked about the show. He was definitely handsome, strong and apparently well-mannered, but he didn't interest her. A brush of air against her neck caused her heart to skip a beat. Casually, stretching her neck, she looked up to see Ware standing at the railing on the deck above. God, he was handsome, even when he looked so stern. She returned her gaze to Michael. Maybe Ware was upset she was in the presence of another man, but if he hadn't kept her pheromones blocked for so long, she could have met men before being with him and Nase.

Stubbornly, she concentrated on Michael. There had to be other men who were right for her and wouldn't betray her.

* * * * *

There weren't any men right for her, at least not on this ship. Erin straightened her new dress as she stood in front of the mirror in the bathroom of the nightclub. She was too much of a wimp to go back to the suite, so she'd bought a few items and changed in Adam and Len's cabin.

Maybe it was just this particular venue. After all, it was a couples-only nude cruise, so how was she to find a man interested in her? But what if it wasn't the venue? She had a sinking feeling it would always be like this for her. Was she destined to compare every man to Ware and Nase?

Or had she found "the one" on her first try? Rather "the two." God, she didn't know anymore. They had forced a life of masturbation on her for eleven years. How could she forgive that? How could she forgive the years of wondering what was wrong with her, of trying to please everyone? A lot of good that had done.

Stepping out into the darkened club, she sidled along the wall and slipped outside. The club was on Deck Ten near the front of the ship. The moon was almost full and reflected off the ocean. She watched the waves move the silver light, making it sparkle. They would make dock in Key West in the morning and then the following morning they would disembark in Ft. Lauderdale.

She leaned on the railing. Then what? Back to work. Back to her condo her sister had used. Back to her friends she had left who used her to make plans for them. But not back to Ware and Nase. They would go to their home somewhere in the sky. She looked at the stars. Which one was their planet? Could it be seen from Earth?

A familiar brush of air on her bare shoulder that purposefully moved down her arm had her closing her eyes. She wouldn't look for him. She refused to react. The air stopped and she released the breath she held until she sensed him. He was right behind her. How could she know that? She couldn't. She was imagining things. Ware wouldn't approach her. He always respected her wishes, always waited.

"Erin."

She opened her eyes, but couldn't form a word past the lump in her throat. It couldn't be Ware. He was patient, in control, and would never push her.

Two warm, masculine hands cupped her shoulders. "Bedia, look at me."

She let him turn her around to face him, his masculine nakedness overloading her psyche. Her heart yearned for him even as it ached. "You need to leave me alone."

"No."

"No?"

His mouth touched hers before she could form a thought. His tongue pushed open her lips and invaded her mouth. The scent of the tropics had her limbs melting.

He ended the kiss. "I want you. I want you with my body, my heart, my mind and my soul."

His green eyes reflected the silver light of the moon, making them glow, but his words seeped into her heart where they cuddled the hurt he had put there. "Why did you do it to me?"

He cupped her cheek. "I wanted you to be safe. I never realized how it affected you. In our world, the years go by slower. I didn't know you were hurting. Ah, Erin, if I had known I would have freed you. We made a mistake. One we will always regret, but we did it out of love. We never meant to hurt you. The pain for us is crippling, knowing how much you hurt because of us."

She pulled away, his naked body too distracting. "I can't think straight when you are near. Leave me."

Ware pulled her into his arms, and she opened her mouth in shock.

"I cannot let you go. I waited too long before. I will not do so again. You belong with us. I can't control this." Ware's voice shook as a tremor ran through his body.

That he tried to keep himself from her and failed was reflected by the pain in his eyes. She couldn't keep him at bay any longer. He hurt, and her own heart couldn't bear it. "Ware."

As his mouth came down on hers, she wrapped her arms around his neck and kissed him back with all she had. Love blanketed her as desire ignited. When Ware pulled back, she gazed at the love shining in his eyes. Of course she would compare every other man to him and Nase because they were "the ones." Who could compete with that?

Ware stroked her back. "Will you forgive us?"

She ran her hand through his long, silky hair and his lids lowered. "I think I can forgive you if you promise to make it up to me."

His eyes snapped opened and she smirked, hoping he could see she was joking, somewhat.

His lips quirked until he smiled. Then threw back his head and laughed.

The sound sent shivers racing along her skin and filled her with joy. Being enveloped in Ware's arms at the moment she made him laugh was heaven.

When he looked at her again, his smile was still in place. "You are special, Bedia. We knew that when we first saw you. We will spend the rest of our lives showing you exactly how much we appreciate you, if you will let us."

She stilled. "Wait. Are you asking me to marry you?"

Ware looked over his shoulder and upward.

She followed his line of sight to see Nase on the deck above, his hands gripping the railing so hard she was surprised it hadn't broken. "Nase."

At her voice, he threw his feet over the banister and jumped down the full story to their deck.

She sucked in her breath, ready to go to him, but he pulled out of his crouch like a panther and joined them. She lifted her hand to his face. "You waited."

"Only for you. I would wait another eleven years if I had to." His seriousness was such a change. What was happening here?

Ware shook his head again. "If we had spent time with you sooner, I wouldn't have waited four seconds. Nase, I told Erin we would like her to spend the rest of her life with us."

Nase pulled her hand into his and kissed it. "Will you?"

Oh God. They were serious, but it wasn't the typical marriage proposal. She was being asked by two amazing men who lived on another planet. "What about my job, my family, my condo, my—"

Ware squeezed her. "Bedia, the practical aspects of life we can handle. The question is, do you love us?"

Did she? Her chest warmed. She had thought them too good to be true and then they proved they were fallible in a big way. How could she not be satisfied with that? Not only were they incredibly attractive, honorable, respectful, and intelligent, but they loved her. Her.

"Erin?" The worry in Nase's voice came through loud and clear as did the concern in Ware's gaze.

She held their hearts in her hands and she could never let them break. "Yes, I will."

Nase's yell was loud enough to be heard inside. "The Poetess be praised!"

Erin laughed.

Ware grinned before Nase pulled her out of Ware's arms and gave her a ravishing kiss that woke every pleasure point in her body. Being held in Nase's strong, naked embrace stoked the fires.

The doors from the nightclub opened and Adam came out. He walked toward them cautiously. "Erin? Everything all right?"

She pulled out of Nase's arms and hugged Adam. "Everything is wonderful. Thank you." She kissed him on the cheek.

"What was that for?"

She moved back and took Ware's hand in her left hand and Nase's in the other. "I found the ones."

He grinned. "You are one lucky lady."

"Oh, I know."

Chapter Twelve

"Naked? Everyone is naked!" Erin dropped her purse and stalked across the living room of her condo. "You couldn't have told me this sooner? What else aren't you telling me?"

Ware and Nase looked at each other for a moment before returning their gazes to her.

There was more. After a week of having them at her place, she'd become much better at reading them. She'd also discovered her roomy condo shrunk when two large Edenists stayed with her.

Now she could understand why they'd had a suite on the cruise ship. They needed room. The last day of the cruise while docked in Key West had been magical. They'd gone to a nudist bar, made plans and drank margaritas then returned to the ship to make love and hit the midnight buffet.

When she returned home, she'd had a month to make all the arrangements they'd talked about in Key West. She had missed them terribly which reinforced that she had made the right decision. This last week they arrived to help her with the final details. Yet in all that time, they never once mentioned the dress for Eden was *undressed*.

"Fiya, we told you we lived near a naked city when we first met you."

"Yes, but that's when I thought you meant the nudist town in France. I didn't know that meant people live naked on Eden. You never told me that."

Again the two looked at each other. Coming back to her couch, she threw herself on it. "Okay, I'm not going anywhere until I get all the facts. Tell me about this naked city."

Nase plopped down on the chair facing her and took her hands in his. Ware remained standing by the bay window. "In Naralina, wearing clothes is considered rude."

"Don't people get cold? What then?" She couldn't help remembering the older lady on the cruise ship. Even she had a shawl against the air-conditioning.

Nase shrugged. "I've never been cold."

Ware joined them, leaning his hip against Nase's chair. "When people feel chilled, we use Hestas. They are blankets. The material is very thin and see-through, but it is quite warm."

"Oh." So much for wrapping herself up in a blanket.

"Of course, for special government occasions we wear arm bands and hats and all sorts of ceremonial things." Nase grimaced. "When we ruled there—"

"Wait. Ruled?" She looked from Nase to Ware. Were they some kind of royalty now?

Nase sighed. "I'm sorry. I didn't realize we hadn't told you. Naralina has what you would probably call an oligarchy-type government. Five kindred rule the city together. Ware and I were from two of those and on the Ruling Circle."

Okay, so now she had to wrap her head around the fact her two "agapaytos," as they said husbands were called, were in charge of a city. No, had been. "You said you were. So if you aren't now, does that mean you were voted out or what?"

Nase looked at Ware. Ware uncrossed his arms and sat next to her. He didn't touch her though. "We were banished."

"What? Why?" She looked at him and then Nase and then him again.

"We were not vigilant enough."

Nase let go of her hands and stood. "Right. Ware thinks we were supposed to suspect everyone all the time of plotting behind our backs to make us look as if we planned to break the law."

"You were banished because you looked like you were planning to break the law, but not for actually breaking it?"

Ware scowled. "The Criuson Law is older than the Dickinson Laws and has been adhered to by the entire planet of cities. It would be the same as if your government discovered someone planned treason."

The idea of her two men doing something against their laws was so preposterous she had to wonder about the people in Naralina. Then again, there was corruption in her own country as well. "So what did you do?"

Nase started to pace. "We left the city before they could throw us out. I think it made us look guilty, but Ware was worried they would remember our portal chips and remove them. If that had happened, we would never have been able to come to you. We didn't want to take that chance."

"How long ago was this?"

"Five years."

"And you live in the jungle now? Is that difficult?" Would she be giving up her creature comforts for a Tarzan-like environment? If so, she wanted to know ahead of time, so she could prepare mentally and physically.

Again the men exchanged looks. Ware sighed. "Yes, it is difficult because I fear for your safety."

She tensed. "Wild animals?"

Ware's brows lowered in confusion. "Yes, we have wild animals, but most are not a danger. The danger is because the lawbreakers of Naralina are banished from the city, no matter their crime."

The concept was so foreign to her, it took a moment to understand. "So instead of jailing your criminals you send them away?"

At Ware's nod she couldn't help admiring the idea. So no one paid to incarcerate them and if they survived it was on their own. But conversely, were not the people in the city prisoners? Obviously, there would be a lot to learn.

Wait. Ware and Nase lived in the jungle. Now she understood Ware's hesitation. "So why now? Why were you willing to meet me and hopefully bring me home?"

Nase came back and sat across from her. His eyes lit with his excitement. "We have built our own compound. It's its own city. All the comforts of home are inside and while we were away, the wooden walls were reinforced with cyndistone."

"How could you do that while you were away?"

Ware laid his hand on hers. "Not by ourselves. We have befriended many in the jungle who we discovered were also falsely accused and judged. We did not realize until recently, that there are hidden factions ridding the city of those who get in the way of their plans."

She pushed her hair behind her ear and focused, trying to understand. "What are their plans and why would you be a hindrance?"

Nase rose suddenly. "We don't know."

Ware squeezed her hand. "One of the many reasons I was hesitant to bring you home."

"And now?"

Nase stepped behind Ware. "Now, we can't imagine living there without you for one more day."

She moved her gaze to Ware. "Is this true?"

"It is." He placed her hand over his heart. "We want you with us."

She laid her own on top of his, the Dickinson poem coming to mind. "Futile the winds to a heart in port. Done with the compass. Done with the chart."

Nase shouted, "By the Crius. You're right!"

She smiled, barely holding back the tears of happiness at the love she'd found. "Then what are we waiting for?"

He smirked. "For you to take off your clothes."

* * * * *

Erin stared at the beautiful white stone city that rose behind golden walls. It was truly breathtaking, reminding her of Minus Tirith from *Lord of the Rings* because everything was pointed, only this city was accented with gold. But that was fiction and now she stood before a very real city on a very real planet. It was almost too much to take in.

Ware stood next to her, and she felt his pride and happiness to be back on Eden. Glancing at him, she was rewarded with a view of his smile as he looked upon the city.

Nase squeezed her hand. "It's beautiful, isn't it?"

"Yes, it is."

Ware's mood changed faster than going from zero to light speed, and she sensed it. Even before he opened his mouth, she felt his heartbreak. Why did she know that?

He looked at her, his face serious. "Unfortunately, we cannot take you there."

"But someday." Nase nodded once, his expression stern. "We will return and take back the city and then you will see all she has to offer. But for now, we have lingered too long. You are not safe until we get you behind sturdy walls."

Seeing this take-charge side of Nase was revealing. At her condo he had often laughed, and was even more relaxed than when he was on the cruise. When she'd donned her running shorts, sports bra and sneakers to come to Eden, he'd simply smirked while Ware tried to literally talk her out of them, but she'd persevered… this time. Her men were gloriously naked, but since they arrived on Eden, she had yet to see Nase smile. Then again, they had only been on the planet for fifteen minutes.

"Our compound is not far, about three Earth-miles. We dare not use the portal any closer in case the Naralinians have discovered how to track portal openings beyond the city walls. We don't want them to know our location, but there are many criminals out here so we need to be quiet." As he spoke, Nase moved forward, his hand firmly gripping hers. Ware fell into step behind her. She had to admit, she did feel protected.

The jungle was a vibrant green with such a large variety of plants, she wished they could take their time, but there would be other chances. At least she hoped so. As she brushed by one bush, she admired what looked to be a foot-long caterpillar with a white-and black-striped body and an orange head. It reminded her of something she'd see in a cartoon, not an actual living— "Ow!" Before she could even touch her face, Ware had scooped her into his arms and Nase spun around. "What is it? Oh no, does it hurt?"

Erin moved her fingers from her cheek and there was blood. Just great. She was barely on the planet twenty minutes and she'd already cut herself. "It's okay. I think it scared me more than harmed me. It stings, but I'll live…unless the plant with the bright-purple flowers is poisonous."

Nase shook his head. "No, not to humans."

"Good." She lifted her top and wiped her cheek. "Ware, you can put me down now."

He made one of his noncommittal grunts, and gently lowered her.

Nase took her hand again, but moved a little slower. She determinedly kept her eyes ahead of her.

After mere minutes, Nase halted. "We're being followed."

Erin listened for sound, but it was such a new place to her, she had no clue what was normal and what wasn't. Ware stepped up and plastered himself against her, his concern seeping into her consciousness. As if on cue, Nase quietly disappeared into the bush.

She turned to face Ware and his arms came around her, holding her close. She kept her voice low. "What is it?"

"I don't know, but Nase will find out."

"It's my fault. If I had just watched where I was going, I would never have yelled. Now we may be followed."

Ware stroked her back. "No need to worry. We will take care of you."

That sounded heavenly. She let her face rest against his bare chest as she kept her eye on the spot where Nase disappeared.

"It's not good." Nase's voice sounded behind her.

Erin jumped. Ware's hand on her back stilled, and her heart pounded.

"How many?" Ware's voice belied his tension.

"Many. Too many to count. And they're organized. It didn't sound like they had been expecting us. They just got lucky." A look passed between the men and Erin felt Ware's worry.

Nase pointed. "We will need to run for the compound unless you want to use the portal."

Ware shook his head. "No. Naralina was too close to detecting this technology when we left." He looked at her. "I know you can run. Follow Nase and go as fast as you can. I will pace myself behind you."

She swallowed. She didn't even know what the threat was, but Ware's fighting instincts were up and that alone put her on edge.

He turned her around and pointed up. "See that treetop with the double branch?"

She scanned the horizon and found the tree he indicated. "Yes."

"That's where we are headed. If anything happens, run toward it."

She stopped breathing for a moment. This was serious. What had she been thinking to come to another planet? For all she knew, there could be something in the air that could kill her.

Ware's hands on her shoulders started her breathing again. His own breath whispered past her ear. "You can do this. We aren't far."

His belief in her helped. He wasn't just saying those words. She could actually sense his confidence in her. Was it the planet that made it possible to suddenly understand Ware's emotions? If so, then why didn't she feel it around Nase?

Nase stepped up to her. "Are you ready?"

She took a deep breath. "Yes."

"Let's go."

Nase ran and she kept herself no less than two strides behind him, not sure if he held back or not. When the sounds of the movement in the undergrowth on either side of them caught her attention, she found herself right on his heels. "Move."

He picked up the pace and she matched him. She had just glimpsed the top of a teal-colored wall through the trees when Nase stopped and caught her as she ran into him.

"Ow." That the man remained standing was a testament to his strength, she'd been in a full-out sprint.

His hand tightened around her arms. "It's a trap. They knew we'd come this way."

She looked over her shoulder to see Nase spoke to Ware, who stood behind her. She'd hadn't heard him approach.

Ware nodded to the right. "The savinstone."

Nase took her hand. "Come. We have a plan."

As they jogged away from their destination, she had a strange premonition that all would not be well. Then again, she'd never been right about her gut feelings.

When they broke through an opening in the verdant undergrowth, it became clear what savinstone was. On the edge of the almost circular clearing sat a boulder of gold. That it was worth nothing on Eden was still a bit hard to accept. Nase pulled her into the middle of the open area, which didn't make sense to her. Shouldn't they hide? She tamped down the need to voice her opinion. Her men lived here. She didn't, at least not yet.

Ware stood on her other side. The plant life around the area moved and filled. Naked men stepped into the clearing. Men, no different than Ware and Nase. She breathed easier, knowing it wasn't a contingent of some strange man-eating animals. Still, their intent could not be good if they were all criminals, but that didn't stop her from taking in the view. Every one of them was built for a woman's bedtime pleasure.

A tall blond man stared at them for a moment and then turned and spoke to another man. She couldn't tell what they were saying, though she listened hard.

The tall man took a step toward them. He sported a birthmark on his hip, but it didn't look like Nase's or Ware's. "Hand over the woman and we will allow you to pass."

Ware's confidence permeated her mind. Why would he be confident because they wanted her? She glanced at Nase and was shocked to see him smile confidently before he addressed them. "Sorry, she's bonded."

The man at the edge of the clearing examined her from her cropped top to her sneakers. Then he sniffed the air, and shook his head. "Maybe, maybe not."

Now what exactly did that mean?

Nase looked at her. "Crouch down."

"What?"

"Crouch down." He pulled her down with him as he sat on his haunches.

The blond man's shout to move back came too late. Ware spun in a circle. His ability to push air threw back every man surrounding them. Nase stood, his hand still in hers. "Run."

A surge of adrenaline like she'd never known filled every limb and she found herself keeping up with him. Ahead she could see an open area before the walls of what had to be the compound. They would make it!

A loud crack like a lightning strike sounded and something blindsided Nase. One moment he was there, the next his hand left hers and he'd been thrown aside. In front of her stood a man with brows lowered and muscles bulging. She swerved, but she was too close, and he latched on to her.

As she twisted, he pulled her against him in what could only be called a bear hug, from the size of him.

Nase's growl sounded like a furious animal and new energy rushed through her. With all she had, she slammed her knee into the man's thigh, unable to gain enough leverage for the sweet spot she wanted. He stumbled before falling backward, taking her with him. She wriggled to be free, but his fingers bit into her sides the more she moved.

A shadow fell over her and her captor. She stilled. *Ware.*

"Release her."

The man beneath her tensed. "No."

"You wish to die?" Ware's complete lack of fear helped her relax, but the hard chest beneath her could have been mistaken for stone.

"If I release her, then I die."

Ware's voice remained calm. "Nase."

She looked toward where Nase had flown, but he wasn't in her line of vision. Not much was except the ground and her captor's chest. He also had a birthmark symbol, but it was blurred by scar tissue. A grunt sounded off to her right. At least Nase was still conscious.

"Tell this man whether I speak the truth." Ware's voice rumbled low.

Nase's grumble was clear. "He speaks the truth."

The man beneath her sneered. "So you would say as his friend."

Ware sighed somewhere above her. "Do you not know a truth-reader when you see one?"

Her kidnapper shifted his head slightly. When his hold loosened, she scrambled off him and threw herself into Ware's arms. He held her tight and her heart finally found its normal rhythm.

"Now what, Ware?" Nase approached, a tall man with long brown hair pulled back in a ponytail followed him closely. "You promised not to kill him. So what are we going to do? Let him go?"

Erin pulled back and turned as the man who had caught her stood. He stared Ware in the eye, both being of equal height. He was just as broad, with a military haircut and square jawline, but his skin had many scars and his fisted hands warned that like a cornered animal, he was ready to strike.

As if he could sense her feelings, Ware pushed her behind him. "We need to know his kindred. Nase."

Nase stared at the man. "What is your name and your kindred?"

"I am Jahl and I have no kindred." He spat at the ground.

Ware addressed the man standing next to Nase. "And you?"

"I am Khaos." The man didn't elaborate and she felt Ware's frustration as he scanned the man's body. Why was the kindred so—oh, the kindred hinted at what special abilities they might have.

Nase stepped close to her. "Ware, there's movement."

Ware's only reaction was the hint of a nod as he stared at Jahl. "Turn around and walk."

"What?" Jahl's stoic face fell.

"You will be our prisoner."

Jahl raised his eyebrows in disbelief, but turned and headed for the edge of the jungle.

Ware looked down at her. "Go with Nase."

Before she could say a word, Nase had taken her hand and they followed Jahl. She looked back but Ware had disappeared and Khaos was gone as well.

"Nase, how can this man be our prisoner? We don't even have a gun trained on him."

Nase didn't take his eyes off the man. "There are no guns in Naralina. We use our natural gifts, and we have many. Jahl's only advantage had been surprise and then holding you. Now he has neither, but we don't know his mark, so we must be wary."

"What about his men?" She glanced over her shoulder and spotted bushes moving behind them.

"Ware will take care of them. We need to get Jahl to the compound." As if on cue, they broke through the jungle growth and approached the greenish-blue stone she had glimpsed earlier.

"Halt." A voice from the high wall stopped them. "Are you friend or foe?"

Nase yelled back. "Nase and Ware with a prisoner and our bonded woman!"

Cheering could be heard inside before a hidden door at ground level slid open. A second later, it shut.

Nase spun, grabbing Jahl and pushing him in front of them just as Jahl's men came into the clearing. Anything his men did would effect Jahl first, as she was sandwiched between Nase and the wall. Nase's voice hardened. "Stay where you are."

The men hesitated and the blond man from the clearing approached. He was taller than either Nase or Jahl and had a rather large nose, but his chin looked chiseled from granite, the lines were so sharp. "I am Sandale, partner to Jahl and Khaos. Release him."

Nase shook his head. "He laid hands on our agapayto. We will take him with us."

Sandale raised his hand, but Jahl yelled, "Hold!"

The tall blond lowered his hand and frowned. What was he about to do?

Nase nudged Jahl in the back, but the man didn't take the hint. "Tell your men to leave."

Jahl shook his head at Nase's command.

Energy surged through Erin just before Nase knocked the man unconscious with a strange looking rock. She snapped her gaze to Sandale. His anger was palatable. Nase smirked.

Erin sensed confidence and readiness coming from the trees. *Ware.* How could she feel what he felt? This was crazy. Anticipation flooded her and she dropped her gaze to the men facing them. In the blink of an eye, they were all thrown back with Ware's air-touch. All except one very angry Sandale.

Ware strode toward the man, wary, but calm. "Come back in one cycle of Selene and we will release Jahl."

Sandale's body was like a statue, completely still and tense with rage. What did he expect after attacking them? "This will not be forgotten."

Ware stepped closer and Erin sensed hard anger inside her as he spoke. "No. It won't."

The two men stared at each other a moment longer before Ware stepped around Sandale, strode to them and took her in his arms. "Are you okay?"

She nodded before looking around him to see Sandale moving toward his men, shaking his head at Khaos, who appeared suddenly through the trees.

Nase slapped Ware on the shoulder. "Let's go." Ware took her hand and he and Nase hefted Jahl up and dragged him as the three of them strolled through the now-open door to her new home.

* * * * *

Nase watched Erin unpacking in their bedroom. The see-through drapes did nothing to hide her beautiful body from him. The simple task had him relaxing, or it could be the fine ale he drank. He stretched his legs out and crossed them at the ankles. It was good to be home.

Erin may not want to be needed, but they did need her, and want her, as she preferred. But it was far beyond want now. He loved her with every fiber of his soul. Never would he let her go.

"We are bonded." Ware sat down across from him on a similar silken couch.

"How can you be sure?" Excitement brought his muscles to attention. "We've only been on the planet a full day. Are you sure? I thought it would take longer."

Ware grinned. "I did too, but our planet is working fast. I feel her emotions and she mine. Can you identify your connection?"

Disappointment crowded his thoughts, but then hope ignited. A woman couldn't bond with just one man. Bonding took at least two men. So what was their connection? He shook his head. "No, I can't. Nothing feels different to me."

"I'm sure it will come."

"If she can feel your emotions then her ability to read you could be a significant advantage for us."

Ware raised his brow in question.

"You and I have trained together since we were young, but she has just joined us. That means in any given situation, she would be lost as to what we would do next. But if she can feel your emotions, that will clue her in, help her understand the way we think. It will keep her safer."

"Good point. I'm glad it is so." Ware relaxed.

Nase was pleased to have eased his friend's mind on one account. He took another swig of ale and smirked. "On the other hand, you won't be able to keep anything from her. She'll always know how you feel."

Ware's look turned thoughtful. "Shall we see how well that works?"

"How?"

Ware grinned. "What if we started discussing her many assets? I'm sure a certain emotion would come to the fore."

Was Ware actually playing around? It was too unusual to be real. "So you mean if we talked about how rosy her nipples are or the sweet taste of her pussy and how we would like to both fill her at the same time, that some of your excitement might catch her attention?"

Ware rolled his eyes, even as his hand moved to his hard-on.

Nase looked at Erin. She had stilled. When she turned and gazed at Ware through the wispy curtains, energy shot through Nase. "Holy Crius."

"What is it?"

He laughed, too pleased to keep the joy inside. "I've discovered our connection."

"And?"

"Her energy is linked to mine. She was excited by your interest in her body, which sent energy racing through her veins and made my body race as well."

Ware stood. "I want to test this bonding."

Erin stared at them both. If she sensed his own excitement, making love to her would be a wild experience for her. He wanted to give her that. "Do you think she's ready?"

Ware laughed. "She's been ready for eleven years. We're the idiots who didn't have a clue. Come. Let's go pleasure our agapayto."

Nase stepped forward and stopped.

At Ware's questioning gaze, he simply lowered his head and opened his arm.

Ware moved forward then halted. Wrapping an arm around Nase's shoulders, he pulled him forward and they entered their bedroom together.

Epilogue

Erin floated on her back in what could only be described as a Roman Bath on steroids. For this to be their private bathroom in the middle of a tropical jungle was more than she had ever expected. The look of the compound may be rustic, but it had every modern amenity and she had only seen a small part of it. She couldn't wait to explore every inch of the place and find out what made it tick.

The warm water relaxed her after the rigorous workout Nase had given her at sunrise. He'd made his expectations clear. She would have to learn to defend herself as well as be part of the dynamic duo of Nassic and Wareson. She smiled, completely satisfied to be considered an equal member.

Her only doubt was in not telling her agapaytos about her birth control. Absently, she rubbed her upper arm. The etonogestrel implant she'd had inserted on Earth would last three years. Her lack of conception was bound to be noticed, at least by Ware. Whenever he spoke about children, his face softened and excitement danced in his eyes. Nase, on the other hand, was all for holding off. How strange the two of them were so close and yet could have such strong opposing opinions on children.

But the birth control was the right decision for her. She was on a completely different planet with no hospital in sight. Having a child would be a huge undertaking. She could wait and so could Ware. Besides, there was so much to learn. Later today he promised to show her the security systems for the compound. She couldn't wait to see that technology.

Eden was such an oxymoron of ancient culture and advanced technology from the Crius. She couldn't wait to figure out what her role would be. Her life had made an incredible turn for the perfect, all thanks to a simple poem and a geeky interest in other worlds. She must have done something right.

Desire washed over her like a wave and she started, still adjusting to the strange "bonding" effects caused by the planet. Letting her feet sink to the bottom of the pool, she turned to find Ware leaning against a column. His dark, naked body, even relaxed, was a picture of hard sinew and curved muscle lines. Her own interest peaked. He may be able to quietly sneak up on her, but his emotions now gave him away. "Did you need me?"

He uncrossed his arms and stalked to the edge of the pool. Crouching down, he waited for her to move closer. "I always need you, but right now I want you." The slight crooking of his lips made her heart melt and her pussy moisten.

She laid her hand against his face. "Thank you for that."

He simply turned his head and kissed her palm. Delight shot through her hand and down her arm. Moving her hand, she traced the contours of his chest, following the line down his crunched stomach to the large cock pointing at her. Taking it in her hand, she softly grasped it. The remembered warmth and strength of that part of his body from last night made her desire keen.

She used her other hand to dribble water over his chest. "So are you coming in, or will you wait for Nase?"

He cocked his head. "We don't know the distance yet of this bonding. You did not sense me until I was in here. Nase is with the prisoner at the other end of the compound. He may not sense your rise in energy."

She stopped her strokes and gazed up at him. "What were you feeling as you walked into our bedroom?"

"Feeling? Not anything in particular." He paused. "So you think the stronger the emotion the farther you can feel it? Maybe we should test Nase?"

She grinned and let go of him. "I like that idea."

He slipped over the stone edge and joined her, pulling her body flush against his. The water only covered them from the waist down. Cupping her head, he kissed her, his mouth taking possession of hers just as he had taken her heart. She pulled the tie that held his hair back and ran her hands into it, pressing herself against him.

"Ah Bedia, what you make me feel."

"I know. Can you feel it from me?"

He stopped kissing her and stared into her eyes. "Do you sense what I'm feeling now?"

She gasped as love flowed into her. She blinked back tears. "I love you too."

He cupped her cheek. "I know."

"This is an amazing feeling, but it will take getting used to."

"For me as well. The sense I have around Nase is from years of being together and knowing what to expect and how he thinks.

What you and I have is different. We will all learn and be stronger for it."

"I guess Nase is too far away."

Ware's lips formed a devilish smile that had her catching her breath. He winked. "Let's see how much energy you need to produce to catch his attention."

She wiggled her brows. "Sounds good to me."

"Good." He bent her back and his mouth latched on to her breast. Excitement flared as his teeth nibbled and bit at her hard nub. With his mouth still sucking at her nipple, he pushed her against the wall of the bath. He released her breast and lifted her up to sit her on the wall. Then he pushed her legs apart to reveal her folds to his gaze.

She laughed. "Have you been taking lessons from Nase?"

"No. But that man better get his ass over here fast because I want to be inside you and my gut tells me he wants to be too."

"Then I guess if he is a little late in arriving that could be perfect timing."

Ware shook his head and gazed into her eyes as he moved his hands up her thighs. "No, that would be too late. We want to be inside you at the same time."

"The same time? But that's—oh."

As his fingers parted her labia, her heart sped. They wanted to come into her ass and her pussy. Anticipation warred with nervousness until her skin tingled.

Ware rubbed his thumb against her opening before circling her clit.

Her tension skyrocketed and then doubled. "He's here."

They stilled and listened. At first there was no sound beyond the native birds, but soon they heard footsteps, running.

Ware nodded and she laughed. "You did that on purpose."

"Everything I do has a purpose."

She watched the stone doorway, anticipating the sight of Nase. But Ware didn't wait. Instead he bent over and licked at her clit.

"Oh God." She forced herself to watch the entrance while Ware ratcheted up her need, making her pussy seep with moisture. Finally, her vigil was rewarded.

Nase stepped around the corner and halted. He looked at Ware's head between her legs and then met her gaze, his own so filled with desire that her energy shot up again.

She noticed Nase's chest jump before he strode to the bath and jumped in.

Ware lifted his head. "It's about time you arrived."

Nase growled. "You could have sent a runner."

"True, but it was more fun this way."

Nase pushed Ware out of the way and drove his tongue deep inside her. Her pussy clenched and spirals of need centered in her core.

"Lay back, Bedia." Ware spoke from behind her and she let him rest her head in his lap.

While Nase licked at her clit, Ware massaged her breasts, sometimes tweaking a nipple unexpectedly to send jolts of desire down to meet those Nase caused at her clit. When Nase pushed two fingers inside her, her back bowed with the pleasure.

Nase's mouth began to suck and Ware's touch became constant pinches on her hard nubs. The desire in Ware combined with the energy emanating from Nase sent her over the edge. She cried out in her joy as her body pulsed.

When she came back to earth, she sensed the desire in Ware. How he could hold back when it was that strong amazed her. Just feeling him had her wanting more, wanting him. Nase's energy had her own rising quickly and she sat up. "Thank you, both, but I think it's your turn now."

The double sensory input from the two men made her sway, but she held on to her position at the edge of the pool of warm water.

"Come here, Fiya."

She slipped into the water and into Nase's waiting arms. Within seconds, he'd lifted her legs around his hips.

"Put me inside you."

The buoyancy of the water made it easy for her to hold on around Nase's neck while she lifted her hips. Teasingly, she slowly impaled herself on his hard cock, enjoying the feel of him stretching her to the maximum. She would never tire of that feeling.

Ware's breath on her neck had her reconnecting with his desire. It was so powerful she had to push it away a little. His hands on her ass surprised her, but as he massaged, her muscles loosened. Then his finger found her anal star and she tensed.

"Relax, Bedia. I will go slow to extend your pleasure."

Her heart thudded in her chest at Ware's words, and her pussy contracted around Nase.

He growled. "Lock your ankles around me."

She did as she was told, despite the excitement coursing through her. Ware took advantage of her distraction to push his finger inside.

Oh God, they really were both going to take her. The idea of having them both had her body opening.

Ware's finger withdrew and despite her nerves, the disappointment was real. Her body wanted this.

"Nase, come this way more."

Ware backed himself against the wall of the bath. Then he massaged her ass again, spreading her cheeks as his cock bumped up against her hole.

Nase grasped her hair and pulled her face back from his shoulder, where she'd buried it. "Relax. Let the pleasure come as it will."

She must have looked unsure because he kissed her on the nose before his mouth claimed hers. The ultimate surrender to his mouth, his cock and Ware finally claimed her.

Ware's cock pushed in an inch and she moaned, the need to pump between the two men mounting. Nase held her to his mouth, his tongue mimicking what he would do with his cock soon. The anticipation had her tensing with need.

Ware's voice in her ear calmed her, despite the desire pouring from him. He slipped in deeper and her pussy clenched hard, causing Nase to release her mouth. "By the Crius, this is too good."

She gasped as Ware pushed in the rest of the way, completely within her ass. He pulled them all back against him and she whimpered at the double sensations coursing through her body.

Nase gazed into her eyes. "Are you ready?"

All she could do was nod, her throat too tight to allow any words through.

Nase pulled his hips back until his cock head was not quite out of her sheath and then pushed himself back in. Exquisite vibrations jettisoned throughout her pussy and ass and she yelled.

Nase pulled back again, her pussy sucking at his cock, her ass holding tight to Ware. When Nase pushed back inside she yelled once more, the pleasure too much and yet not enough. The rhythm started and each thrust in sent her shouts to the ceiling and her body into spasms. When she thought she would faint from the sheer bliss, Ware moved too and it set her orgasm off.

Warmth filled her ass as Ware's shout vibrated along the walls and Nase came deep inside her, gluing his pelvis against hers. He and Ware linked arms, squeezing her between them, prolonging the double excitement and satisfaction.

When they could all breathe again, Ware slipped out.

Nase walked with her still attached and gently set her on the steps. The warm water soothed her well-used body.

Ware sat on her right and Nase on her left. They were so much more than she'd ever dreamed of. *Eden* was more than she'd ever dreamed of.

Ware clasped her hand. "Rowing in Eden! Ah, the sea! Might I but moor to-night in thee!"

She grinned as love filled her soul with the words of her favorite poet and her favorite poem. "You are always welcome to moor in me."

Nase squeezed her hand. "Me too?"

"Oh yes, you too. It's funny, I never would have guessed when I fell in love with that poem that Eden was another planet or that I would fall in love with the men who gave it to me."

Ware leaned over and kissed her cheek.

Nase stared at her, one eye brow raised. "Fall in love with us? Fiya, that part was written in the stars."

At his smug smile and Ware's quirked mouth, her heart warmed. There would be a lifetime of living and loving in, of all places, Eden.

The End

Unexpected Eden

The Eden Series: Book 2
Coming Spring 2015

For updates, sneak peeks, and special prizes, sign up to receive the latest news from Lexi at http://eepurl.com/D3MqT

Also by Lexi Post
Masque (http://www.lexipostbooks.com/books/masque/)
Passion's Poison (http://www.lexipostbooks.com/30-2/)
Passion of Sleepy Hollow (http://www.lexipostbooks.com/passion-of-sleepy-hollow/)

About Lexi Post

Lexi Post spent years in higher education taking and teaching courses about the classical literature she loved. From Edgar Allan Poe's short story "The Masque of the Red Death" to the 20th century American epic *The Grapes of Wrath*, from *War and Peace* to the *Bhagavad Gita*, she's read, studied, and taught wonderful classics.

But Lexi's first love is romance novels. In an effort to marry her two first loves, she started writing erotic romance inspired by the classics and found she loved it. Her books are known for "erotic romance with a whole lot of story."

Lexi is living her own happily ever after with her husband and her cat Giz. She makes her own ice cream every weekend, loves bright colors, and you will never see her without a hat (unless she is going incognito).

Lexi enjoys hearing from readers. She can be contacted at lexi.post@yahoo.com or through her website www.lexipostbooks.com.

www.ingramcontent.com/pod-product-compliance
Lightning Source LLC
Chambersburg PA
CBHW070955120726
47910CB00004B/1246